THE LIVES AND TIMES

OF

EL CIPITIO

a novel

by

Randy Jurado Ertll

Published in the United States of America by

ERTLL PUBLISHERS

www.randyjuradoertll.com

Cover illustration by Billy Burgos

ISBN 978-0-9909929-0-5 (pbk.)
ISBN 978-0-9909929-1-2 (ebk.)

First edition 2014

Printed in the United States of America

1 2 3 4 5 6 7 8 9 10

THE LIVES AND TIMES

OF

EL CIPITIO

PROLOGUE

After El Salvador's civil war ended in 1992, I returned to Soyapango, one of the most violent and dangerous places in the world. You had to pay the *renta*, or daily tax, of the local gangs for travel in and out of the area. Those who refuse to pay were murdered.

I worked with *cooperativas* and rode the ruta 7C bus every day from Soyapango to San Salvador, the most dangerous bus ride.

Gangbangers hopped on the bus with machetes dripping blood, pointed guns at people's heads and demanded spare change. Some sniffed drugs and carried grenades. I saw one banger with a human hand, a diamond wedding ring still attached. The owner of the hand had resisted being robbed and the banger decided to simply chop her hand off.

They demanded spare change with, "*Maciso*, help a homeboy" and I gave them one colon. Some had been deported from the United States, speaking only English on arrival. The locals made fun of their broken Spanish and said they sounded like Chicanos. The homeboys were angry that they were perceived more American than Salvadoreños. They could not believe that they had become foreigners in their own tiny country. They would say to each "motherfucker, we are neither from there nor here, que mierda. Somos como huerfanos."

I became used to riding the bus, and loved the fruits and

semillas de marañón sold during the journey. I also bought *agua de coco*, Coca-Cola, and *una Kola Shampan*. I felt at home even though I did not fit into the small seats.

Every day, I saw a small boy wearing a straw hat. He had a potbelly and dark, brown skin of the most beautiful earth tone. He had big brown eyes and Mayan features. But once you looked deep into his eyes, you saw a certain darkness and fogginess that reflected death.

He wore typical *campesino* clothing.

One day the bus was packed tight with passengers, and I had no choice but to go to the back and sit next to the boy. No one else wanted to be near him. I found it strange that he hid his feet. The other bus riders were terrified.

Being a naïve *Salvadoreño Americano* I sat next to him.

As I rode on the rinky-dink bus that smelled of diesel and had a tape player blaring Michael Jackson's "Billie Jean," the boy told me his name: *Soy El Cipitio.*

He began to speak. I had never heard such a voice, and ended up being captivated and hypnotized. Slowly I felt that I was in another dimension with the boy as my guide. The bus seemed like it was sort of floating, as if we were in a different wavelength. The concept of time disappeared.

He told me a magical, fantastic story. Along the way, I fell into a deep sleep, but I still heard El Cipitio telling me a story of extraordinary proportions. I felt as if I was a character in a *Twilight Zone* episode. He gave me a little piece of paper that provided a blueprint for peace. El Cipitio was beginning to repent of his evil ways and he was looking for opportunities to spread a message of hope and peace.

After the bus ride, I never saw or heard of El Cipitio again, but I wanted to share his story with the world. I hesitated to reveal my experience until now. It's up to you to believe it or not.

CHAPTER 1

Fuck it, said El Cipitio, fuck this world. He was born to La Siguanaba, a crazy mom who killed him when he was born. She was known as Mayra before she drowned her son because he was born with his feet backward and brown skin. But El Cipitio came back to life.

He was a crazy little fucker, but not crazier than his big titty mama. Some said she went *loca* after she drowned her newborn son and tossed him into the *quebrada*. Once she realized what she had done, she constantly searched for his little ass. She cried and cried. El Cipitio just wanted to get away from her and start his own life.

He was pissed off that he never aged past ten years old and stayed three feet tall. The demon was devious. He wanted revenge. The rage caused by his mother led him to commit untold tortures and murders. His power came from his eight-inch penis that grew to fifteen inches when erect, also giving him immortality. This was his secret and no one knew about it. Otherwise, they might find the source of his supernatural powers. He had a deep hollow in his heart since his own mother had murdered him. He felt unwanted and unloved. He longed to find the love of his life and end his deep, dark loneliness.

You had the evil El Cipitio, but you also had the sweet El Cipitio, the one forever in love. He stalked beautiful girls and threw stones at them to get their attention, and gave each a

3

small country flower. His favorite fruit was the banana, *guineo majoncho*.

People saw El Cipitio after he died. Being already dead, he teleported his body to any location in the world the pleased. That is why he remained so elusive. He also hid and sought solitude in the gigantic volcanoes of El Salvador. To survive, he ate the ashes. That is where he felt most safe. He could be philosophical in the coolness and quiet offered by the dormant volcanoes. He often thought about his deadbeat father.

El Cipitio was pissed off that he never knew his father. Rumors circulated that it was El Cadejo (or El Coyote), an evil demon with bright red eyes. He could transform himself into any animal he wished, wolf, dog, coyote, or fox, whichever he pleased. El Cadejo had a split personality and sometimes appeared as a white wolf/dog or black wolf/dog.

In fact, El Cadejo was El Cipitio's father. El Cadejo had raped La Siguanaba. The priests of the Catholic Church had done nothing to protect her. Instead, they condoned the rape along with the plunder of the Mayan, Aztec, and Incan empires. A number of the priests took erotic pleasure in seeing the mass rapes during the colonization. They were frustrated since the Church had forced them to take vows of chastity.

Unfortunately, they unleashed their sexual desires on innocent victims and condoned the abuse conducted by the colonizers. The priests were accomplices and the guilt forever haunted their sinful and wicked souls. They knew the rapes were wrong but they did nothing to stop it.

El Cipitio should be glad he never met his evil father. He would have been ashamed of his looks, anyway. El Cipitio fantasized about having a father who looked normal or a man he could be proud of, like a Mayan prince.

He wanted his father to be a proud member of Aztec or Mayan royalty, but all he got was a demon of a deadbeat dad. El Cipitio was stuck with an invisible father that only appeared around midnight to prey on his next victims in the *cantones*, the small rural villages.

El Cadejo was brought on a ship from Spain in 1492. He was on board the original three ships given to Cristobal Colon—*La*

Niña, La Pinta, y la Santa Maria. These ships carried the worse criminals from Spain, many held in cages since they were so vicious and dangerous. El Cadejo escaped from his cage. The fucker was devious by nature.

El Cadejo was considered a serial killer in Spain and he had terrorized Europe for centuries. Once the King and Queen of Spain captured him, they found a great opportunity to get rid of the murderer by deporting him to explore new territories with Cristobal Colon. Colon was in debt and somewhat naïve—he did not realize the King and Queen were using him to transport the deadliest criminals. They believed Colon was taking them to India, but they mistakenly landed on a small island in the Caribbean called Salvador. From that time, the colonization and mass murders of the indigenous population began.

El Cadejo ate half of the men on *La Niña* as it crossed the Atlantic. The other half never talked about it since El Cadejo explicitly told the *hijos de puta*, "If you mention my eating habits, you will be my next meal, with or without salt." The fucker had no decent table manners.

Once the ship arrived and landed on tiny island that they named Salvador (not El Salvador), El Cadejo disembarked and went on a rampage through the Caribbean. He settled in Cuzcatlan (now known as El Salvador) after roaming and creating destruction through what would one day be Central America. For an odd reason, he took a liking to Cuzcatlan. The *Pipiles* had a distinct taste and he liked the smell of their blood. The blood was extra salty.

He created chaos and much violence. The indigenous population, the Pipil and the Natuatl, told stories of a beast-like demon with blood red eyes roaming the *cantones*.

He hypnotized his prey, the hard-working *campesinos*, before eating. Many disappeared and were never accounted for. El Cadejo ate them, and when he was full, he created clandestine cemeteries deep in the jungle. He made necklaces from the bones of his victims that he wore around his neck. He made decorations with bones and sold them in various market places. People thought they were plastic. They did not realize the ornaments were human bones.

El Cadejo stayed young by taking on the bodies of his victims. He mixed with the population at times but the villagers knew El Cadejo was out there somewhere. He had lived for centuries. He was immortal. Eating the bodies and absorbing the energy of each soul gave him eternal life, and helped sustain his strength and power. No one could match his physical abilities.

In 1932, General Maximiliano Hernández Martínez declared war on El Cadejo since he posed a threat to his new presidency. General Martínez feared El Cadejo more than he did his hero, Adolph Hitler. He tried to imitate him since both were crazy and believed in the occult. General Martínez' nickname was El Brujo; he said spirits protected him from any competition.

He wanted El Cadejo eliminated and gave orders to the *Guardia Nacional* to search for El Cadejo. Many military men became victims of El Cadejo. He cooked and ate them with beans and *queso duro*.

That was El Cadejo's favorite meal, chunks of human flesh.

General Martínez was desperate. After years of failure, he asked General Francisco Franco Bahamonde (Franco for short) of Spain for his *Guardia Civil* to train his army battalions and police in finding El Cadejo. They were unable to catch him and the Guardia Civil took much of their rage out on the natives. General Martínez gave the order to kill most of them, known as *La Matanza*. Tens of thousands of natives were murdered. He wanted El Cadejo at any cost, but his men never found or captured him. El Cadejo mixed in well with the population. He was a natural chameleon.

The natives paid a great price. They were targeted, murdered, and hacked to death by the military. Blood flowed through the villages, and the rivers ran red with so much blood. Violence was so intense that nature was disgusted. The natives lived close to the land and when they were murdered in massive numbers, El Salvador's largest volcanoes erupted with fury.

El Cadejo met Mayra, a beautiful young woman who lived in the countryside. She was elected the queen of her village and El Cadejo fell in love. Even demonic spirits fall in love. She was not just the town queen, but ahead of her time as a free spirit who did not want any man to control her. She was known smarter and stronger than any man in her village. Her beauty was deceiving since no one knew the power of her spirit. She did not take shit from anyone and stood up for her rights.

He watched every move of that beautiful woman. He wanted her really bad and found out she had a crush on a local *futbol* player named Luis. That was all El Cadejo needed to know. He began to attend the soccer games so he could check out his competition.

El Cadejo began to fantasize. He saw himself as the local soccer hero, the one to become the national team star and take his team to the FIFA World Cup. He wanted to impress Mayra. He hated the player that was winning Mayra's heart. He had to get rid of him.

One night, he ate the player who might have been a star. El Cadejo took on the appearance of Luis and courted Mayra. They fell in love. She did not realize that an evil spirit had taken Luis' body and he was El Cadejo, the most evil and deceiving, just like Satanas. El Cadejo fell head over heels for Mayra. He loved her silken skin, her perfume smelling of flowers, and her sensuality and eroticism. She had big voluptuous breasts that made El Cadejo forget everything else. El Cadejo cooked Luis with a secret barbeque sauce. The house was filled with the smell of barbeque meat. Both, El Cadejo and Mayra ate the sizzling meat and Mayra said that it was the best she ever had. After eating, they both had erotic, wild sex.

CHAPTER 2

TIME PASSED. EL CADEJO AND MAYRA REMAINED YOUNG. The spells that worked for El Cadejo did the same for her. In 1970, Mayra got pregnant and she knew something was not right because all her family members had died or disappeared in a mysterious manner.

One night Mayra found Luis as El Cadejo, devouring and cooking limbs. He had gone to the local cemetery for take-out. He fried legs and arms with *platanos* and *semillas de marañón*. He loved platanos *fritos*. He did not know Mayra was pregnant.

When she saw what he was doing, she went crazy and headed to the quebrada, the little river stream down the embankment.

She howled in pain as her son was born. Mayra knew she had to do the unthinkable for any mother and drowned him in the deepest part of the river, home to shrimp and soapy water. Of course, she felt compelled to drown the baby for its brown skin, never mind its backward feet. But El Cipitio had a light skinned twin brother. She followed the Spanish influence of discrimination and kept the light skinned baby hidden under her breasts. She had to give him away too.

She thought she had murdered the little demon, El Cipitio. What she did not know was that he came back to life. However, she went crazy from that night on. She came out at midnight to scare every man out getting drunk or being unfaithful.

La Siguanaba, as she was now known, grew long, pointed fingernails that cut like razor blades.

From pain and desperation, her breasts sagged tremendously and she only owned a see-through nightgown. She no longer had tight, voluptuous breasts with small nipples. Her face turned pale as white cotton with deep bags under her eyes. La Siguanaba's hair changed into grotesque tendrils. She no longer looked like the queen of her village.

She cried without any control. Men lost their minds when they saw her. Some committed suicide by hanging themselves or taking poison. She repeated the same statements: "I killed my son" and "I lost my son." Her deep hollow cries made the hairs on the back of your neck stand up and gave shivers in the hot, tropical weather.

Pinche Siguanaba. Porque me aogaste? El Cipitio whispered in her ear, making her crazier. El Cipitio was a vengeful little fucker. He had a vindictive trait he adopted from his father, El Cadejo.

She screamed and replied, *Porque eres el demonio.* El Cipitio disappeared into the fog. He could walk backwards thanks to his crooked feet. They were turned completely around. That was how he deceived his enemies. They followed the footsteps that led them in the opposite direction. La Siguanaba spent countless hours walking along rivers, with a look of desperation and desolation.

He carried pebbles in his pockets collected from a river stream, to toss at the prettiest young women bathing in the water. El Cipitio was a romantic at heart. He fell in love with dozens of women at the same time and liked seeing them in their see-through blue, pink, and yellow *blumeres* (underwear). He was like Hugh Hefner, the founder of *Playboy* magazine, always in love with beautiful women. El Cipitio was a dandy, a natural born player. He wore silk underwear to make his giant penis comfortable and not so sweaty during the hot summer months, and gloves with soft cotton inside to keep his hands clean.

Since El Cipitio had stopped growing at three feet tall and stayed ten years old forever, he disguised his age and made

9

himself look taller by wearing a typical campesino straw hat he received as a gift. He had a bloated belly from beans, farts, watermelons, and *lombrises*. El Cipitio loved *frijoles monos* and *sandias* from the farmers. He ate a whole sandia in one sitting, and poured salt on it too. Deep down he longed to be a farmer so he could grow his own platanos. He loved guineos mahonchos. They were his favorite. That was how he survived the times of starvation in El Salvador. He carried an extra mahoncho is his pocket, but his dick was bigger than all the platanos.

He suspected his father was El Cadejo and they each avoided each other. El Cadejo killed for pleasure; El Cipitio tortured and murdered for survival. He had two halves, one trying to do good and the other one full of the evil he had inherited.

El Cipitio walked through the countryside eating *jocotos*, *marañónes*, *chipilines*, and anything else that looked appetizing. Once in a while he would steal a few pupusas made of loroco, revueltas, and the ones with cheese and beans were his favorites. While he devoured the food, he would inhale the pure smell of beans grown by the campesinos. While eating, he saw young men and women training in guerrilla warfare. They were novices too clean-cut to know how to use weapons. He also saw campesinos carrying more than machetes or *cumas* to work the land. They had AK-47s.

He stumbled on gringos near the cemetery, Vietnam veterans training army battalions on guerrilla counterinsurgency. In the late 1970s, American soldiers taught the new death squads torture and effective mass murder techniques. The soldiers also worked as sales representatives for corporations that sold weapons and bombs to developing nations in Latin American, Asia, and Africa. They created the need for more weapons to be bought. The greater the internal strife meant greater profits for the corporations. It was in their best interests for different civil wars to break out around the world.

They sold many weapons to guerrilla groups, even to Fidel Castro and Che Guevara in the 1950s.

The generals came up with the term, "The Cold War," and

pitted capitalists against communists. It worked and millions of weapons were sold.

Some American and Salvadoran soldiers saw the little kid with the straw hat and bloated belly. El Cipitio appeared normal, but they did not realize he was the son of El Cadejo, and half kind and half evil.

He was the eternal *enamorado.* The other waited to be discovered.

CHAPTER 3

ONE DAY IN SAN MIGUEL, EL CIPITIO STUMBLED ON THE Batallón Díaz Arce. They recruited him. He was the youngest member and they figured he could clean their boots, carry their water, and grease their M-16s. They did not know he could murder every one of them with his pinky finger.

El Cipitio seemed like a kind, loving, and friendly boy who liked to play with butterflies, dragonflies, and hummingbirds, unable to break or steal the little hummingbird eggs. He was split down the middle after being shot in El Salvador. The bullet from an AK-47 went into his forehead, through his brain, and exited through the back. Everyone thought he was dead, but El Cipitio came back to life. He was part of the walking dead. This injury caused, deep, throbbing head-aches for El Cipitio. He would say esta*"mierda! dolor de cabeza."*

Soon the Batallón Díaz Arce taught El Cipitio how to cut people into pieces, electrocute them, cut off ears and pour lemon juice on the wounds, stick needles in the pupils of the eyes, strangle, and burn people alive. One soldier called El Machetero taught El Cipitio how to strangle, suffocate, and chop people's head off with one swing. Another soldier called El Negro, showed him how to do waterboarding and other means of suffocation.

At first, El Cipitio hated the training, especially from the gringos who did not speak Spanish. He hated that they made fun of his straw hat and potbelly. In his mind, he recited, *"Estos hijos de puta me las pagaran."* His Mayan blood rejected the colonizers.

El Cipitio sharpened his hatred, revenge, and self-loathing. He developed his rage. The campesinos were being tortured and he did not enjoy it since he was also a campesino. American soldiers told him to feel superior since he was from a special breed of *mestizos*. They nicknamed him the little Mayan prince. His job was to teach the *indios* how to behave and act. If they were suspected of being subversives, they were tortured and murdered. He referred to other mestizos as *"estos indios ignorantes y rebeldes."* El Cipitio began to see himself taller, lighter skin, and naturally superior to the *indios* and mestizos. He would imagine himself as el cacique that had to control and humiliate his own people. He imagined himself to be gentleman Spaniard – with tons of stolen gold. He also developed a secret little yellow book – *a librito amarillo,* where he would write the names of his victims. He put little starts next to the ones that he would enjoy torturing. He got the idea of creating such a little book, by reading Chairman Mao's little red book.

The anger over his mother drowning him and having a demon for a father gave him an internal frustration waiting to blow up.

In 1980, the civil war exploded and the countryside became hell. El Cipitio could no longer walk around and flirt with the prettiest women. Most were being tortured by the death squads and murdered. The army battalions also kidnapped girls and boys, and sold most of them on the black market to corrupt international adoption agencies. It was a big money maker. Some of the campesinos would simply say, "se llevaron a los cipotes." The others went to human trafficking gangs. El Cipitio's girlfriend, *Tenancin* was one of the little girls that was kidnapped and never seen or heard from again. He always felt a deep, pure, love for her. Rumors circulated that she may have been adopted in Italy.

El Cipitio had a twin brother he did not know existed. His name was El Duende. Since life is fucking crazy, El Duende fought along with the guerrillas. La Siguanaba had him alive. Out of every possibility, El Duende signed on with

13

the communists. You cannot get more ironic than a cold war between twins, yet the circumstances were common during the civil wars in Central America. Family members fought each other in the wars. Many were forced to fight. They did not have a choice.

El Duende fought in the war as a child but never met his own brother since he stayed in Santa Ana and El Cipitio in San Miguel. He was also born with certain powers and could hypnotize people by whistling. He enjoyed eating human livers and tongues. His secret weakness was an allergy to bee stings. These could lead to death. El Cipitio was born with the same allergy but he would not die. If he did, he eventually revived.

During the civil war, El Duende grew tired of being used to construct bombs, launch rockets, and serve as a *comando urbano*. He did not like how the *comandantes* bullied him.

He decided to leave the guerrilla cell since he had already learned every subversive skill. He was a top comando urbano. His trainers nicknamed him El Cherito, in reference to him being "our little friend." They were amazed at how nimble, fast, and devious El Duende had become, and proud he was the youngest comando urbano. El Duende could do back flips and swerve to avoid bullets and bomb shrapnel.

That fucker fought in the mountains and on the streets of San Salvador. He used the special powers from his evil dad, and sometimes read people's minds. He was able to enter their souls.

He got tired of the comandantes giving orders to the poor peasants. El Duende remained his own man and knew he was stronger, smarter, quicker, and more courageous than all the comandantes put together. He would never be promoted to comandante since he came from a working class family. Most of them came from the middle class and had a high school or university education. The comandantes gave the best jobs to their close friends and family members. *Puro cuello.* Many avoided taking part in actual fighting. They were afraid to be murdered. Their role was to be intellectual and lead the masses. The comandantes would fantasize to become official politicians and taking over the Presidential palace. They had seen how Castro took over the government. They wanted to emulate him. Some of the comandantes knew that if they would win the war, then they would have access to the best wines and women of the country. Some secretly admired Rafael Leonidas Trujillo, known as El Jefe, from the Dominican Republic since he could get the finest women once he became President. Also, they admired that Trujillo was a staunched environmentalist who protected natural resources and green space. Some of the rebels dreamed of having convoys of big, black, shiny cars that were bullet proof. They saw how the Central American Presidents and their Generals drove around town with 20 other armored cars that served as security. It was also done to impress the local women. They wanted not to just emulate, but actually, become the new elite or oligarchy. Deep down inside, they knew that they were lying to themselves and to the masses, ultimately what they wanted was recognition, power, money, and women. Their dreams included dressing in silk and smelling like roses and vanilla.

No mobility existed for El Duende within the guerrillas, so he decided to immigrate to the United States. Where he lived was a secret; some said Washington, DC, and others claimed Virginia, or Maryland. El Duende was seen roaming the forest areas, climbing trees like a monkey. He loved taking naps within the leafy trees.

Another rumor had El Duende moving to Griffith Park near Hollywood, and joining the *Dieciocheros,* or 18th Street gang, to be their most effective killer. Glimpses of him were caught partying on Sunset, San Monica, and Hollywood Boulevards. He loved the underground scene and hanging out with the Dieciocheros. He liked the gothic crazies and male prostitutes that walked around Hollywood shirtless in tight-ass jean shorts. He attended satanic clubs at night. El Duende was at ease around the outcasts.

He made fun of the male prostitutes in their Pro Wings tennis shoes and fake Levi's shorts. They used Krazy Glue to attach stolen Levi's labels on the left pocket of their jean shorts. They were proud to wear fake originals. The jeans made them look sexier and attracted better paying customers. El Duende liked them since they knew how to party, smoke weed, and used heroin. They had to be fucked up since their customers were ugly as hell and smelled funky too.

El Duende worked part time as a Domino's Pizza deliveryman to learn the concept of creating franchises. He stole the company secrets about the structure of Domino's and followed them step-by-step in establishing different clicas near their locations. The crazy fucker was so creative that he devised an innovative concept to deliver pizzas and *pupusas* via Domino's. He stuffed the pupusas with various drugs that were delivered to the clicas, who then sold the drugs. The male prostitutes were the best sellers and consumers. Politicians, police officers, and teachers knew where to get the good shit— from El Duende. He thought of creating a union to represent the male prostitutes but he knew they would say, "Fuck that shit. We're not gonna pay union dues to the fat cats."

Even the police and military had a piece of the action. El Duende learned from Domino's that tipping is critical in keeping your staff happy. So, he tipped the different police officers and soldiers. He bought good will, and set up shop next to the Armed Forces recruiting office on Sunset Boulevard.

El Duende was deported in the 1990s and replicated his business plan in El Salvador and all through Central America. The police and military admired his entrepreneurial skills. Generals requested private meetings with him to discuss how U.S. aid could buy more weapons, and then sell them at wholesale prices to the Dieciocheros. It was a perfect plan for the generals to become instantly wealthy. El Duende said, "Hell yes, motherfuckers. I will buy the weapons from you but they have to work." He planned to overtake and conquer *Mara Salvatrucha,* or MS 13, the transnational gang with members from California to Mexico to Central America. He did not know that his twin brother was *el mero mero* of MS 13. El Duende would take naps, and imagine destroying and eradicating MS 13. His dream was to become the only *mero mero.*

There is some truth when they say twins think alike and do similar things.

16

CHAPTER 4

A BOUT THE SAME TIME, EL CIPITIO DECIDED TO WALK through Guatemala and Mexico and up to El Norte. He wanted to explore nature since he loved the writings of John Muir and the photographs of Ansel Adams.

El Cipitio had heard that El Norte was beautiful and dark skinned boys like him could become millionaires and through their wealth be seen as very good looking. He figured many *cipotas* would fall for his charm in El Norte. He was very self-conscious and hated being dark skinned since his mama had drowned him for his skin color and crooked feet.

He fantasized about wearing fancy tennis shoes instead of homemade sandals. The wealthy boys in San Salvador wore American tennis shoes, jeans, and fancy shirts, especially Polo and Le Tigre shirts. The girls swarmed over them. El Cipitio wanted to be the dandy of every woman.

He had to hide his demonic side inherited from his father, and his clinically insane mother, La Siguanaba, who continued to roam the rivers and roads. He wanted to get away from that shit.

In Guatemala, El Cipitio took buses and trains. He met wonderful people that looked like him, and could relate to his Mayan side. His father, El Cadejo, had murdered many of the natives and wanted to be Spanish. He hated the natives so much he contributed to mass murder in 1932. Of course, no one ever knew it was El Cadejo. They blamed General Martínez.

He walked through Mexico and saw how Central Americans were brutalized, beaten, raped, and murdered. It brought back memories of what Batallón Díaz Arce did in his home country. The guerrillas and death squad members acted meek and humble while crossing Mexico, but they were beasts to their own people. They learned from their Spanish masters during colonization to hate women, and beat their wives, mothers, daughters, and girlfriends.

The army battalions pleased their U.S. military trainers by showing them how they could torture without mercy. They said with great pride, "*Mire jefecito, como le corte los dedos y las orejas,*" for approval and acceptance. The gringos never saw them as equals, only mestizos trained to torture and kill their own, but they claimed the murders were necessary to destroy communism. Most campesinos did not know what communism was about. They merely asked for fair wages and respect. El Cadejo did not tolerate any grumblings about rights. He was a fucking tyrant.

He wanted to be Italian, not Spanish. El Cadejo liked fine wine, cheeses, and to dress like royalty. He detested anything less. That is why he rejected and denied his son—he came out short, with a potbelly, and native looking. He preferred his son to look like a little northern Italian boy with blonde hair, blue eyes, and grow to at least six feet tall. El Cipitio was only three feet tall, with brown eyes, thick black hair, and fingernails full of farming dirt.

El Cadejo would have murdered his own son but La Siguanaba did it first.

He was a wanderer and only left La Siguanaba pregnant like a typical mujeriego that only used and exploited women. El Cadejo offered no child support. Cheap motherfucker. He was truly a deadbeat dad, the same as the thousands of men who were proud to impregnate women and leave them. They believed the movies on television. They thought that having many children across the country was a badge of honor. They did not think about how the children suffered and went hungry and carried a deep emptiness through their lives.

They did not think of the traumas and anger their abandonment instilled in the children. Being tossed aside by an uncaring father created hatred in the children, and the need for revenge. The children developed rage and fury that became uncontrollable.

Without a father, thousands of Salvadoran women were forced to leave their children with their grandparents. They also decided to come to El Norte to work, and avoid being raped or murdered in their home country during the civil war. Unfortunately, many were raped while they crossed Mexico on foot. The coyotes, military, police, and drug traffickers took advantage of the women.

The children of these brave mothers were left as orphans in El Salvador.

El Cipitio was too proud to see himself as an orphan. He saw himself as a man of action, *un chingon*. He picked up the word in Mexico, and he liked it. He wanted to be the biggest and baddest *chingon* once he arrived in *los Estados Unidos*. El Cipitio chose not to use his powers while crossing Mexico unless provoked. If attacked, he easily killed anyone.

He made a promise to let no one fuck with his fellow mestizos, and defend instead of torture them. El Cipitio had a weakness: guilt and shame that tormented him on a daily basis. He even wrote a poem:

I fuck with you, you fuck with me.
They fuck with me, we fuck with them.
You better not fuck with me,
'Cause I don't give a fuck.

El Cipitio was a poet at heart. He wrote love sonnets, haikus, and had talent to compete with Chile's Pablo Neruda. He wrote secret love poems to the prettiest women in town. They found the poems placed in their bras and did not have a clue how they landed there. El Cipitio developed many crushes while he crossed Mexico and Guatemala. He was mesmerized with many women he met along the way and wrote poems for them.

When they read the poems, the women were soon warm and tingly. Some fell in love with their secret admirer. They daydreamed about the poet and had erotic dreams with Prince Charming.

They did not realize he was a little fucking three-foot tall, potbellied fool. The women that would read his poems fell in love with his words.

He carried a notepad for when he was inspired to write his love poetry. He was the eternal lovebird and imagined being bigger than Don Juan Tenorio. He wrote poetry to good-looking nuns and tried to romance the Jehovah Witnesses and Mormons while they tried to convert him. He had no limits.

El Cipitio thought about converting to the Church of Latter Day Saints in order to marry many women at the same time. He loved that interpretation of the Bible, for the convenience for men's self-interests and sexual desires.

But he needed to keep moving. He could not settle down and become another Jim Jones, insane cult leader of the People's Temple in Jonestown, Guyana. He knew he would be discriminated against for being so short and having a *Guanaco* accent.

A la gran puta and *hijo de la puta* would likely get him into hot water. He pretended to be Mexican while in Mexico. He told people he was an illegitimate son of singer Joan Sebastian, and Vicente Fernandez, another musician, was his uncle. No one believed him, so he claimed to be the illegitimate son of wrestler Mil Mascaras.

He felt terrible being treated as an undocumented immigrant by the *federales*, who always stole the *colones* – *bolas* and *semillas de marañón* he carried in his pockets. They treated him like a little bitch. He would later begin to use a code word in reference to Mexicans, he would call them los mariachi.

When a Mexican immigration agent tried to rape El Cipitio, his El Cadejo side came out. He tied the rapist and grabbed a machete, and chopped him into little pieces. He made a big pot of *menudo* and invited many federales and immigration agents to come and eat, with Dos XX beers for everyone to drink and enjoy what they ate. Once everyone had a buzz, El

Cipitio said he was a guanaco. They could not believe it and decided to name him "an honorary Mexican." That was the highest honor the Mexicans could give a Guanaco. Deep down inside, El Cipitio began to dream of running for political office. While everyone drank their beer, shouted, and played Vicente Fernandez in the background, El Cipitio decided that he would become a crusader for justice.

El Cipitio took pleasure in chopping up that fool. Each blow was for everyone who had been harassed, beaten, and raped. He dedicated the murder to the thousands of children exploited by the *polleros* and the coyotes who sold them into the slave trade. El Cipitio was a child himself and had read the Universal Declaration of Human Rights, and knew about the so-called protection of children in foreign countries from his travels as an immigrant. The Universal Declaration was just a long piece of bureaucratic paper written by policy hacks and attorneys to extend their United Nations consultant contracts. Mexican officials laughed at the mention of human rights for Central Americans.

Such manifestos were a joke. Reality was much different in comparison to lofty human rights organization dreams and goals. El Cipitio had seen how the U.S. was complicit in training children to become death squad members.

His friends were recruited to be part of the Batallón Atlácatl, started in 1980 by the School of the Americas, since children served as spies for the military. The guerrillas recruited children to fight in the war and infiltrate the military too.

Back in El Salvador, El Cipitio was the youngest colonel to lead Batallón Díaz Arce. He was worse that Chucky. He patrolled El Playon, a volcanic lava bed where dead bodies were dumped. After a while, no one questioned El Cipitio's leadership skills. A gringo gave him a video player to show the movie *Patton* as motivation for his troops before they headed out to destroy and plunder villages. El Cipitio thought it was funny that Patton had a squeaky voice.

He wanted to instill discipline into his troops, so he tortured guerrillas in front of them. El Cipitio enjoyed showing he was a master of torture. He was like a surgeon when cutting ears, noses, and fingers. He most enjoyed doing electrical shocks. His troops laughed to see the little fucker run current through testicles and women's breasts and clitoris.

They had never seen such a committed leader. He wore a gold cross and black clothes while conducting his torture rituals. He played the role of an evil priest who mesmerizes his followers and does not condone or tolerate any questioning. Sometimes El Ciptio was so evil that he requested his men to attend mass. Deep down inside, El Cipitio enjoyed the Catholic/Christian music. But of course, he could not show weakness or a tender side.

What a fucking hypocrite. And he loved it. He had inherited the sadism of the colonizers.

Chapter 5

T HE CATHOLIC CHURCH TAUGHT HIM DISCIPLINE AND loyalty when he served as an altar boy. He used some of the skills in his leadership as a colonel. He was only three feet tall but his men feared him. They knew that once he put on the black clothes and the gold cross around his neck, it meant he was thirsty for blood.

El Cipitio commanded his men to capture vultures and drain their blood, and drink it like it was warm milk. Technically, milk is blood anyway.

Vulture blood gave strength and long life to him and his men. He ordered them to eat the bodies of those they had murdered. They also ate crows, since the birds carried evil spirits.

He gave them orders and they had to follow. Otherwise, he fried them or cooked them into *sopa de frijoles con carne*. Yes, he was ahead of the movie *Highlander*. Each person he ate gave him a longer life. The little fucker was advanced. The smell of frijoles took El Cipitio back to his childhood. He loved eating tender chunks of human meat. He had no scruples.

Soon he tired of killing and eating people. His soft side poked into his conscious. He wanted to leave the tiny country. He read history at night while the battalion men slept, so they did not know he was literate. He projected an image of brutality and ignorance, and told his men he could not read or write. He said literacy was Shakespearian bullshit, and life had already taught him everything.

He manipulated his men through violence and they did anything he wanted. He brainwashed them with nationalism. He said they were special guanacos chosen to keep their people in line, and the communists were subhuman and needed to be taught a lesson. He gave the men a sense of belonging and importance they never had before.

The gringos told the battalion men that if they followed capitalism, McDonald's planned to open in El Salvador. Ray Kroc, the CEO, guaranteed free Big Macs and hamburgers to the men in exchange for protecting their country and helping the U.S. fight communism.

El Cipitio's men wanted to work at McDonald's and eat free hamburgers for life. Ketchup never ran out at McDonald's and the company paid for the free air conditioning.

They imagined serving blonde haired and blue-eyed female customers in bikinis. The women ordered large Coca-Colas and gave them notes with their home telephone numbers before they left. The notes said, "Call me, baby." As the former soldiers read the notes, they looked up and said, "Thank you, baby."

The battalion men decided that killing children and innocent campesinos for jobs at McDonald's where they could eat as many hamburgers as they wanted was worth the fight. The imagined smell of French fries mesmerized the soldiers and their true desire was to drink Coca-Cola while they had sex. They thought that the caffeine and sugar would help provide stamina and longevity to have multi hour sex sessions. They ultimately wanted to become love machines.

They dreamed of burgers and blondes every night.

El Cipitio wrote his poetry at night. He had developed a drinking problem and stole dozens of beers from the towns they invaded. He drank them by himself and never shares. He loved pilseners, *supremas*, and sometimes got lucky by finding a *Regia*. He loved an ice-cold Regia; it was better than imported Corona or Budweiser. El Cipitio supported the national beer and stayed loyal. He thought of making his own beer, with an image of himself dressed as the Indio Atlácatl on the label. The fool had creativity.

The problem was that when he drank, he became violent and evil like his dad, El Cadejo. The romantic poetic side disappeared and instead of writing love poetry, he ate his victims. He forgot about his mother and demonic father when he was drunk. Sort of. He simply numbed himself to sleep.

Fuck, when he woke up with a *goma*, or hangover, he was a mean motherfucker.

This was 1980. He got tired of killing, torturing, and burning humans alive so he headed to El Norte.

Once he arrived in Los Angeles, the little crazy fucker moved to East Hollywood to be near the action. He figured he could get a movie deal and earn enough money to publish his poetry. Being known as a published poet attracted many women. Once a player, always a player.

He had seen many Hollywood movies and knew he was better than Robert DeNiro in *Taxi Driver*, since El Cipitio had actually driven a taxi in El Salvador and many of the prostitutes were his friends.

El Cipitio knew he could have won an Oscar if he had played a role in *The Godfather*. He was a dreamer.

CHAPTER 6

H E ENROLLED AT LE CONTE MIDDLE SCHOOL AND WAS the shortest kid in his class. A particular teacher, nicknamed Mr. D, took a liking to El Cipitio. The students called him Mr. D. No one really knew what the D stood for; it was a subliminal message. Some referred to the teacher as "dickhead." He liked taking the kids camping, but not one spoke about what happened during the trips. They came back mute and walked funny.

El Cipitio knew Mr. D wanted his virginity. El Cipitio was too smart and had seen too much. He had killed and eaten people, but was terrified of pedophiles. He hated them so much he refused to cook and eat them.

He dressed like the other kids in school and let his hair grow long, and he was perfect. He wore black to represent his satanic side, and was invited to join the heavy metal locos.

Every time he walked to school through Mid-City Stoners gangbanger territory, the *cholos* made fun of him and called him *mojado* and *chaparro*. He did not mind being called a mojado, but chaparro was an insult. They did not realize El Cipitio was tougher than anyone in their gang.

He was an undercover Andre the Giant, a secret Mil Mascaras, but the MCS *cholitos* did not know.

El Cipitio started *enamorando* all the girls at Le Conte. They called him *el enamorado eterno* and *el poeta sin barrio*. Man, did that piss him off. He wanted a barrio. He did not like the *cholos pelones* who made fun of him in front of the prettiest girls.

He began to think and figured, fuck it, we will borrow part of the name from the Mid-City Stoners and call ourselves la Mara Salvatrucha Stoners, or MSS. He went to the local public library and researched copyrights, and sent a request for "Mara Salvatrucha Stoners" to be registered in the Library of Congress. He tried consulting an attorney at Figure It Out Yourself Legal Services but never got an appointment. The telephones were always busy. He also tried getting through Don't Get Evicted Legal Aid Network without any luck.

El Cipitio copyrighted the name by spray-painting it on his school's restroom wall, where the *placa* has remained. The janitors tried to get rid of it by different methods and even called Bob Vila, the carpenter, to come and help. No matter what, the name never faded because El Cipitio added drops of his blood to the paint. It was demonic from the beginning.

His eyes were bright red when he spilled his blood for the name. He played "Holy Diver" by Dio as he painted and blasted the song in his Walkman when he confronted any MCS cholos. He carried a .38 pistol.

He recruited twelve members: Rambo, Dracula, Pitufo, Gasparin, Cuete, Satanas, ET, Black Sabbath *o el* Blackie, and the acculturated Silent, Trigger, Boxer, and Killer.

El Cipitio had his new battalion, but an urban battalion with urban soldiers. He gave the order, *directo*, meaning a direct hit to the head. He wanted to send a message and decided to hit the shot caller from MCS – he was known as Boxer. He shot him in the head and chopped it off to show his new *mara*, MSS. He was like a proud Samurai. With one swoop, he took the power from MCS. The cement soaked the blood of Boxer. It slowly ran down the gutter. The smell of the dried blood made El Cipitio shiver. He loved it.

A home-girl nicknamed Angel from the rival Clanton 14 Street gang (C 14) was an angel to El Cipitio. She had light brown eyes that reminded him of the *chibolas* he used to play with in his village, back in the home country.

She had beautiful wavy hair and light skin, silky and

smooth. El Cipitio wanted her as his *morra - su ruca*. Angel looked like a Saudi Arabian princess.

El Cipitio started to talk like the local cholos, mainly Mexican American. He called his friends "homeboy" and "*ese*." Slowly, he transformed from his immigrant heavy metal look to a cholo. He began to look like the founder of MCS - Boxer, since had taken his soul when he cut off his head.

His deep-seated hatred came from the time MCS homies stole El Cipitio's shoes in the summer. He walked home without shoes and burned his feet. El Cipitio adopted the habit of stealing shoes from his victims. He did to others what was done to him.

In the process of killing so many rivals, he became a hoarder of shoes.

He had set up different clicas in different areas of Los Angeles. He merged the smaller gangs such as Street Criminals, Black Diamonds and others into MS 13. He wanted a monopoly. He sent Black Sabbath to the Westlake/Pico-Union area. The established gangsters cut his throat in front of a 7-Eleven, the first casualty for El Cipitio.

He went into a rage. He wanted to know who did it.

El Cipitio swore to avenge his friend. He adopted death squad tactics of surveillance, target, and murder. When necessary, he gave orders to eliminate whole families. Soon, headless bodies, arms, and legs were discovered in different places around the City of Los Angeles. The Los Angeles Police Department (LAPD) never made the information public since it was so gruesome and sure to create public panic. The Mayor wanted to be re-elected, and asked the Chief of Police to keep the information hidden since the crimes only occurred in the ghettos. The Chief responded by saying, "They are doing us a favor by killing each other."

The white LAPD cops did not care about Latino on Latino or Black on Black violence. They laughed when they arrived at the crime scenes, and did not offer a cup of water or any resources such as therapy or psychiatric services to the survivors. At times, they called *La Migra* to deport them, since many were undocumented.

Many gangsters and innocent civilians were tortured and murdered in the 1980s. El Cipitio felt like he was back home. He created different clicas and they paid homage to him. He was independent from *La Eme*, the Mexican Mafia, and refused to pay taxes to them.

He had a black attitude when he hung out in South Central Los Angeles. In the disguise of a *paletero*, he built networks and alliances. He set up meetings with leaders from the Bloods and Crips and he signed peace agreements with them – they signed their names on a napkin agreeing to a cease fire against each other. He learned this skill from Norton Renquist, who had forced Republican leaders to sign agreements and pledges not to raise taxes. El Cipitio figured that if Norton had achieved that with a professional mob, then he could do the same with Bloods and Crips. He was seen as a simple street worker and the Crips and Bloods took a liking to him.

They called him "the little brown homie," and others referred to him as "Tiny" without knowing he was bigger and stronger than any of their gangs. He smoked weed with them in the alleys off Figueroa. They jacked off together as they looked at porn magazines.

He became known to the local prostitutes who noticed him selling *paletas* so often that they started to like him. The women taught him American street slang. He was in the bilingual program at Le Conte, but the streets gave him English on a daily basis.

One of his favorite words was "motherfucker." He would sell a paleta, and when a customer asked, "How much?" he replied, "Fuck, motherfuckers, they're fifty cents." He had an attitude and started to be accepted and seen as part of the 'hood.

El Cipitio was the shot caller in Hollywood. Every gang had to ask him for permission to sell drugs in the area. Word got out: do not fuck with the little motherfucker.

The leaders of the La Eme, James Morgan known as Cocolizo, Chayanne Cadenas, and Luis Flores, requested a private meeting at King Taco in East LA. El Cipitio was defiant, and ordered and ate a *burrito de carne asada*. He started to fart. Often. La Eme were impressed with his careless attitude. They could not believe they were negotiating with a little motherfucker that was three feet tall and ten years old, with the audacity to fart as he pleased.

Cocolizo told him straight out he had to pay taxes to La Eme for his kid's college tuition. El Cipitio was surprised that Cocolizo looked white instead of Mexican, and spoke better Spanish than the Chicano homies. Cocolizo told El Cipitio that they had originally started La Eme as an education organization called Ejercito de Mexicanos Educados (EME). They would teach new inmates how to read and write. But that the prison guards helped in making them a prison gang. They would place bets when they would pit Blacks to fight Mexican or Chicano prisoners.

El Cipitio had finally met someone who had an attitude like his: I do not give a fuck and I can kill and eat you any time I want. He ordered a *horchata* and was furious with the results. That shit did not taste the same as the ones he bought at El Mercado Central. It tasted like fucking milk.

He said, "I am full, and I ain't paying shit to y'all," and walked away from the meeting.

The next few years were the bloodiest. Hundreds of MSS soldiers were killed. Survivors entered the prison system to be raped and murdered.

El Cipitio had to negotiate with Cocolizo. His main request was to meet at a Salvadoran restaurant where they sold real horchata.

Cocolizo said, "All right, homie." Cocolizo was intrigue and one day decided to visit a Salvi Restaurant to order horchata. He went to the first Salvadoran Restaurant located on Pico in the sweat shop area of downtown Los Angeles. He had to order from a metal stand. He said "quiero un horchata" and he also request a "platanos with frijoles and crema." Cocolizo could not fucking believe it. The horchata was delicious. He became a fan of Salvi food and wanted El Cipitio to provide to him secret recipes.

He had permission from the board of directors of La Eme to negotiate. Cocolizo talked about his ancestry and said

Aztecs and Mayans should unite. He told El Cipitio to pay $1 million in back taxes and be forgiven, and promised to shut down the green light on MSS. Cocolizo also threw in a freeby for El Cipitio – he would put in a good word with the Aryan Brotherhood (AB) regarding El Cipitio. Cocolizo also liked El Cipitio since he reminded him of the three feet tall undead children of Hungary and Bulgaria. Cocolizo use to play hide-and-seek with them. Some of these kids were able to bench press 500 *lbs* - without breaking a sweat. Some could even bench that much with one arm.

El Cipitio agreed to pay the back taxes. La Eme made him an honorary member and he included the number 13 in his gang name. The Mara Salvatrucha Stoners were soon known as MS 13. Mayans and Aztecs finally decided to support each other. They knew that the Spanish had used the different Inca tribes to destroy each other. El Cipitio would read every night. He wanted to read every single book that the Library of Congress had in relation to Latin American and World History. He knew that knowledge was power.

Aztecs and Mayans had many things in common. They agreed to stay out of each other's way, and attack common enemies together.

El Cipitio soon got tired of gang banging and tried to figure out what to do next in life.

CHAPTER 7

HE OFTEN WONDERED ABOUT GROWING UP WITH A REAL family. He imagined having a blonde mother who cooked pancakes for him.

She hugged and kissed him, and told him how proud she was.

El Cipitio explored why mestizos wanted to be white. He thought about how General Patton had brainwashed him through the movies.

Hollywood portrayed Anglos as caring and loving fathers and mothers, while Latino and black mothers and fathers were shown as uncaring and unloving.

It was true in his case, but he also saw how some of his friends had fathers and mothers that did not abandon them.

The civil war in El Salvador had created those divisions in the families. Thousands of Central American women risked their lives by coming to El Norte, and eventually work in the sweatshops. Many would be mistreated and raped while heading to El Norte.

Conquistadores came from Spain to destroy the native populations, and the devastation had continued for centuries after their departure. He read books about the Holocaust and how Jews were forced to work and made profits for multinational corporations while being held in concentration camps.

He learned from his homies in the Crips and Bloods about

slavery. They told him about the house slaves and how certain ones were chosen by their owners to oversee, beat, and maintain control over their own people. The stories reminded him of the police or *cuches*, the Latino cops that loved to harass the kids in the barrio and served as oppressors for the white man. Some believed they were white when wearing a blue uniform.

He saw black executives who had turned their backs on South Central driving their Mercedes Benz in Westwood but never visiting where they had grown up.

He learned about history, sociology, and political issues while being a paletero. He browsed used bookstores and bought books on revolution.

After he read books by Chairman Mao Tse-tung, Ho Chi Ming, and radical African leaders such as Marcus Garvey and Malcolm X, he decided that his role was to reconstruct his own country, the one he contributed in destroying. One of his other goals was to fix the ghettos of Los Angeles.

He had to change the institutional racism and structures created to keep minorities down.

El Cipitio figured it out while he was a paletero. The whites took the land from Native Americans and exiled them into reservations. The treaties were never respected or honored. He knew the land taken from Mexico was done by brute force. He also read with great interest about *Toypurina*, a Native American young lady who led a rebellion against the colonizers of San Gabriel in 1785. She was eventually imprisoned and sent into exile so that she would not continue to inspire a rebellion.

He was so intrigued by *Toypurina's* brave story, that he visited the San Gabriel Mission to see where the Gabrielino Indians were forced to convert to Catholicism. Some ran into the San Gabriel Mountains to maintain their identity, culture, and religious beliefs, and still live there. They choose to remain invisible. He saw a fire where they danced, cooked, and celebrated Mother Earth. Junipero Serra had never captured them. They developed secret underground tunnels, an incredible architectural achievement.

El Cipitio wanted to be a mixture of Che Guevara, Simón Bolívar, and José Martí. The problem was that he had never visited Argentina, Venezuela, or Cuba. He figured injustices were universal and that they crossed boundaries and geographic areas.

He said, "Whatever, bitches. I am taking on the world."

El Cipitio planned to expose the fake motherfuckers getting rich off the poor communities, and the bureaucracies that used taxpayer money to repress and exploit. He represented the simplicities of life. He founded and created the U.S. Hispanic Leaders Chamber of Commerce. Each member had to pay one million dollars to be an official member. He also created an advisory committee for the Chamber of Commerce that included the wealthiest individuals from various Latin American countries. They were purposely made to be invisible since they would eventually get juicy contracts for import and export products, obtain approval from the U.S. government for airline creations. These Latin American billionaires, who many had become wealthy through the drug trade, would eventually invest in start-up U.S. corporations. Many would invest in building stadiums and in investment firms that were heavily supported by U.S. congressional members and U.S. Senators. El Cipitio had learn the art of politics, which is to make enough money to buy off people. But he kept his Latin American billionaire club advisory group a secret. This offered a slush fund for his political ambitions. He had to portray himself as a man of the people.

He led by example and touted his campesino roots, his humbleness of selling paletas, and his denouncement of material wealth and greed. He showed his austerity by renting a small apartment, and only owning a few clothes and an old car. Other social movement leaders lived in opulence. They collected money for the cause, but it went into their private bank accounts.

Why should a progressive leader live in a mansion or own a fancy home while supposedly representing the needs of the working class? El Cipitio did not go as far as Fidel Castro, who required his people to work in the agricultural fields and cut sugar cane.

He did not want to imitate other leaders. He wanted to be

his own man, like Gandhi but with an attitude and some mean ass, thick, black hair, the campesino hair that never falls out. He said to his friends, "Have you ever seen a bald Mayan or Aztec? Hell no."

The little motherfucker.

CHAPTER 8

E L CIPITIO FASTED FOR SIXTY DAYS WITHOUT CHEATING FOR immigrant rights. He led marches to denounce police brutality. He hated the *puercos*. At a press conference in front of the mansions of corporate polluters, he brought toxic chemicals to make his point. He held fracking experiments to see if the method caused small underground tremors.

He boycotted Wal-Mart. The family of Sam Walton asked El Cipitio to become their spokesperson but he refused, even after they offered him $500,000 per year to say how wonderful they were. He despised how Wal-Mart workers did not receive fair wages or benefits.

He stopped eating at McDonald's because the gringo promises never came true. His friends who worked at McDonald's never earned more than minimum wage and had no health benefits or pensions. The worse fucking part was that not one blonde ever gave them her phone number asking to be called.

That pissed off El Cipitio and drove his rage. He wanted to also expose and denounce the pedophile priests and doctors. A friend had gone to the hospital for a sore throat and a former basketball player doctor with long fingers conducted an ass check. That pissed him off too.

He took on over one hundred social causes. He fasted, marched, and served time in jail for failing to disperse at a

36

protest. He considered lighting himself on fire but did not want to imitate the monks who protested the Vietnam War.

El Cipitio wanted to be original and protested global warming by climbing Mt. Everest and fasting for sixty days. Few people were able to climb the mountain to witness his fasting.

He took on mythic proportions. Stories circulated about him not being human but an extraterrestrial. That pissed him off. He was no ET. He was a committed leader of the masses who lived like they did, in rundown apartments with barely enough food and no savings account or million dollar investments in the stock market.

He was a poor motherfucker.

Exxon, Marlboro, Enron, Exide Battery Recycling Plant and other major companies offered him cash to shut him up. El Cipitio did not accept the donations that could have gone toward his social causes. He was tempted, but he preferred to eat beans and hardboiled eggs. He did not want lobster or bottles of Malbec wine. He enjoyed the simple things.

When he climbed down from Mount Everest, a small child waited for him with a white rose to show his appreciation for El Cipitio safeguarding and protecting white roses in China. He had become an international figure.

His activism had resulted in being more widely recognized than the President of the US. He had higher approval ratings than any world leader. Small countries invited him to participate in their parades and he refused. He did not want attention. He even turned down being grand marshal for the Rose Parade. The attention was unnecessary. He rather chose to just sleep overnight on Colorado Blvd to observe the Rose Parade the next morning. He wanted to be among the poor who could not afford to pay for the reserved seating to view the Rose Parade. He even roasted hot dogs to give away. The fucker was generous.

Mr. Rogers was a much better fit.

El Cipitio grew tired of activism and fighting for social justice. He wanted to do one last major act of kindness. He flew to the Middle East for a meeting with the Jewish leaders from Israel and the Palestinians. He wanted to broker a Middle East peace agreement. No one thought he could achieve such a goal.

But El Cipitio had extraordinary powers inherited from his mother. Before she went crazy, La Siguanaba was the town negotiator, diplomat, and peacemaker. El Cipitio had that gift from her.

He met with Prime Minister of Israel and the Minister of Defense. He gave them *una peperecha* as a gift. They were amazed with the texture, color, and shape of such bread. Once they ate it, they could not stop eating and talking about world peace. The secret ingredients in the bread worked. They made the eater renounce violence. One of the key ingredients was holy water that was imported from the Vatican.

It was a bread of peace. He took the other peperecha to the Palestinian leaders. They ate it and drank coffee. They were amazed with the taste too. The Palestinians were euphoric and wanted to begin dialogue with the leaders of Israel as soon as possible.

El Cipitio was asked for mass-produced peperecha so it could be imported immediately to all of Israel and Palestine. United Parcel Service airplanes flew millions of loaves to the Middle East. El Cipitio had a business side and managed to include in the contract that he earned $1 from each peperecha sold. He donated the money to the United Nations.

The people in Israel and Palestine loved them. They ate peperecha and put down their weapons.

The leadership for both sides sat and signed a peace agreement, and the people partied for three days and three nights straight with zero violence. They crossed borders and danced with each other.

The Pope gave a thumbs-up. He flew to Palestine and danced with the people. Once he ate the peperecha, he also became a full-time advocate of peace. His guilt grew so much that he ordered the Vatican to return the gold illegally taken from Latin America in the 1500s. The Pope had been reluctant but after eating the peperecha he agreed. El Papa told El Cipitio "you are an inspiration."

The amount and weight of the gold was tremendous. The US Navy had to be brought in to take the shipments to the Americas.

El Cipitio met privately with the Pope and requested the returned gold be invested in building thousands of schools throughout Latin America, and that books, paper, pencils, and school uniforms be provided free to each and every student living in poverty.

Once El Cipitio had achieved his goals, he returned to the United States and applied for a job at Homeboy Industries. He wanted to learn how to bake.

While baking one day, he met the cholita named Angel again. He fell in love.

He listened to Kenny Chesney's song, "Me and You," over and over again. His only problem was that she was going out with a gang intervention counselor named Mr. Coca, and having an affair with gang taskforce detective, named Mr. Barrio, from Newton Station. The gang intervention counselor gave her cash and the detective gave her free weed.

El Cipitio was hurt. He listened to Culture Club's "Do You Really Want to Hurt Me?" while baking. He wanted La Cholita to hear the song and the message.

He wanted to become normal and settle down, but La Cholita was a wanderer and a *mariposa*. She liked to be poked by many. No disrespect; she was a true player who told the homies, "Don't hate the player. Hate the game."

El Cipitio was obsessed with her bleached blonde hair, black eyebrows, and tight ass jeans that gave justice to the term, *cinturita de gallina*.

He had renounced violence after peperecha helped create world peace, and learned to bake that special bread himself. He fed all the LA gangbangers. They sat in circles at Homeboy Industries and sang "Kumbaya, My Lord," Los Bukis love songs, and Juan Gabriel's classic *"Querida."*

They sang "Querida" at the top of their lungs.

During his time as a baker, El Cipitio started to drink more beer and the fine wines that people gave to the song circles. He was addicted to fundraising events that gave away free beer and wine, and other kinds of alcohol. He smoked weed and tried angel dust.

He hit the bottle every day while La Cholita kept giving him the cold shoulder. He threw stones at her and wrote his greatest poetry dedicated to the angel.

La Cholita liked tall, buff guys who took cash from donations, and cops who took weed from drug busts. He did not meet her qualifications. She hung around with violent homeboys and El Cipitio was too mellow, slow, and nice. She liked the homies that had conducted drive-by shootings before eating the peperecha.

She got hot and horny when the men killed others. She loved to see blood spill. She smiled when the homies were shot down. La Cholita got hot and bothered, and asked her lovers to play the video, *Faces of Death*, while they screwed. She loved to see people eaten by crocodiles and torn apart by lions, and especially cannibalism. That made her cum.

El Cipitio had fucked up in being a man of peace and La Cholita had no clue he had eaten and digested hundreds of people. She did not know about his violent past and the basis of his power, his penis.

He wanted to be accepted through his poetry, not his violence. He thought about having leg implants to be taller, but any surgeon would see his huge penis. That was his biggest secret. If only La Cholita gave him a chance, he would show her how well endowed he was. He was tired of masturbating to the image of La Cholita. He wanted the real deal. However, El Cipitio had to be careful once he exposed himself to La Cholita. He would have to make sure that she would keep it a secret. That his extraordinary powers laid within his big dick. If someone were to chop it off – he would lose immortality.

One day while baking, he decided to get the fuck out of the there and forget La Cholita. He figured, *ojos que no ven— corazon que no siente*.

CHAPTER 9

H E ROAMED THE STREETS AND EXPLORED THE HISTORY OF Los Angeles, its architectural and engineering accomplishments.

He saw the divisions between the rich and the poor. The rich lived comfortably on the Westside and other areas, while the poor took the slums.

He decided to run for mayor and change things from the inside. He hired his friends, Panzon, Quebadro, Tornillo, and Truco, and set up a professional search committee to find the most qualified instead of those who had contributed the most or worked in previous campaigns. He avoided hiring just beautiful women and *GQ*-looking men.

His team reflected the faces of Los Angeles. He hired an indigenous-looking staff, like the people he had met in Guatemala and Southern Mexico, from states like Yucatan, Guerrero, and Chiapas, not the blonde Latinos and Latinas in the soap operas.

El Cipitio as mayor of the people promised to be bigger than Fiorello La Guardia, mayor of New York City during the 1930s and 1940s. With El Cipitio, the Department of Child Support Services would no longer target and criminalized unemployed parents.

Cleaner than Mayor Tom Bradley, El Cipitio avoided having sexual affairs with his donors. It was difficult and he had a Post-it note in his back pocket to remind him, "Do not fuck the donors."

The Chief of Police Puerco and his officers could no longer continually harass poor community members and target activists. El Cipitio knew about the illegal activities the LAPD did on various activists. The police purposely followed activists, placed drugs in their cars and homes, and planted weapons when necessary. When they knew an activist had certain addictions, the officers made sure he had free and full access. They wanted to record him or her snorting cocaine or fucking bitches at cheap motels. They loved the Marion Barry type of mayor. Instead of doing their jobs, they searched for their next hit of crack or fuck buddy.

A politician like that was easily bought and sold. All it took was one video or audio recording, and they were fucked. When necessary, the police used devious plots like sending undercover agents dressed as Mormons or Jehovah Witnesses for access to a politician or activist's home. They also paid the cable installer and telephone and gas company guys to drop small gadgets that recorded any conversations.

Efficient methods had to be utilized.

For destroying an activist, the cops paid hookers for entrapments. They sent big-ass blondes to seduce them.

It was and is so easy to fuck up the activists.

El Cipitio made sure none of those illegal activities took place in his campaign. He wanted to be an ethical politician and leave a tremendous legacy. What a fucking dreamer.

He wanted huge statues, buildings, bridges, and plaques with his name in bold capital letters—Mayor Cipitio—so he was remembered more than President John F. Kennedy or Abraham Lincoln. He wanted to liberate his people like Moses.

El Cipitio thought he should be equated with Jesus Christ or Allah. His ambitions were larger than his dick. His ego was bigger than Mt. Everest.

One day La Cholita might realize how huge his heart was and he could give her a little sexual healing.

El Cipitio adored Chairman Mao and wanted to implement his accomplishments and strategies at the local level. He figured the only way to bridge the wealth gap was to merge capitalism and communism. Not as easy task, but possible.

During his campaign, he made that his top priority and the masses loved it. He promised that no one ate filet mignon unless everyone could afford it. Community police patrols were planned in West LA, the Valley, East LA, South LA and every other neighborhood to make sure they did not smell the cooking and juices of filet mignon unless everyone had one. It had to be equal. Beef producers were assured of becoming filthy rich by forcing equality and every LA resident able to afford a filet mignon.

The big cattle ranchers loved El Cipitio so much that they contributed millions of dollars to his campaign. They gave him all the free steaks he wanted. El Cipitio felt guilty but figured, what the fuck. He needed the cattle ranchers in his pocket to win the election.

Petroleum industry leaders gave him free gasoline for life. El Cipitio did not give a fuck how much a gasoline cost. He became so bold that he purposely allow over a gallon to spill on the ground when he filled the tank of his old car.

To please the environmentalists, he promised to plant over one billion trees. The masses could eat the mangos, cherries, and pears from the trees free of charge. The voters loved his ideas and his rallies were massive. The cowboys, polluters, and environmentalists loved him.

El Cipitio evolved into a cult leader. The other candidates were jealous of his original ideas. They began to plot and joined forces to destroy him.

One candidate named Panzon said, "Let's use the classic playbook and get someone from his own community to fuck him up." That had worked during the colonization, thanks to the contract services of La Malinche. She was the greatest consultant the Spaniards had hired. They got a deal from her since she did not request a pension or retirement plan.

They hired a professor named Rata to get close to El Cipitio, as his closest adviser on the North American Free Trade Act (NAFTA), mining, and small businesses. The professor was actually a Central Intelligence Agency (CIA) agent.

The National Security Agency (NSA) gave the professor the duty of recording every conversation with El Cipitio.

When El Cipitio got drunk privately, he talked shit and showed his gangster background. Every other word was a bad word. The professor loved it. He had hundreds of hours of El Cipitio talking shit.

He turned over the tapes to the candidates who had hired the NSA to provide private investigation services. The candidates loved the recordings and pissed on themselves when they heard the taped conversations. They were laughing so hard.

El Cipitio suspected someone had betrayed him. He read about Judas in the Bible. He knew he was paranoid and reached out to Cal Tech in Pasadena to counter the efforts of the NSA.

A young Chinese student nicknamed Mao was hired to develop computer software to track traitors and spies by satellite. The student was efficient and loved the fact that El Cipitio admired Chairman Mao. They had many things in common.

Within a few days, the student determined that the professor was the spy. El Cipitio was pissed and wondered what to do. He paid two rogue police officers to shoot and kill the professor. The professor had gone to a strip club and gotten drunk. When he drove through Pasadena, the police stopped his car and made fun of him. They told him his Ph.D. came from bribing the approval committee. That pissed him off, and took off his seat belt and swung open the door of his environmentally friendly car. He reached in his pocket to pull out the degree when the rogue cops saw their opportunity. They shot the professor in the head. In the police report, the cops wrote that he reached for his waistband to pull out a gun.

The cops carried a small shiny gun in the trunk in case they had to frame someone. The professor was easily framed. No one gave a fuck about his being murdered by cops since he was a Latino professor at Cal State. For teachers at an Ivy League university like Harvard or Yale, the President of the U.S. requested the Attorney General to conduct an investigation.

El Cipitio figured the hit was justified. He still had a little gangster in him.

Eventually, El Cipitio won the election. His age was questioned and he proved he was thirty-five years old with a fake identification card he bought in South Central Los Angeles. He was mature and intelligent; his IQ was double in comparison to his competitors. Age discrimination was irrelevant, and the rumors of him being only ten years old stopped circulating. He was so suave, mature, and intelligent, everyone believed he was over thirty-five years of age.

He capitalized on his height by saying his heart is what counted, not being three feet tall. He kept the size of his penis a secret during the campaign. He did not want distractions.

The crowds loved his idealism, enthusiasm, and charisma. Mayor Cipitio was a self-made man and everyone was inspired that he came from selling paletas in the streets of Los Angeles. Who else knew the issues better than Mayor Cipitio? He knew the gossip too.

His first year in office, he hired the top policy people and seasoned community organizers who had not sold out. He tracked their salaries and hired only those that made $20,000 or less per year. They knew the struggles of the working poor and could not be bought off with fancy lobster dinners. They were used to beans, rice, and faucet water. Even if the water was contaminated, they drank from the faucet since imported water from New Zealand was too expensive for the die-hard community organizers. They also believed in supporting the local Department of Water and Power (DWP) since they had generously donated to after-school programs in the inner city.

The organizers could have gone to work for DWP to have credit cards and order fancy dinners with wine justified as business meetings.

Mayor Cipitio interviewed them personally. He wanted to see what was in their hearts. When he had a good vibe from them, he hired them on the spot.

The DWP never ran out of money. They took ten cents from each customer every month. That added up to hundreds of millions of dollars that were pumped into a private foundation.

The top administrators of the foundation and the CEO of DWP wined and dined at LA's finest restaurants. They had regular tables reserved and the wine never stopped flowing.

The Rapid Transportation Department (RTD) was a little jealous. Their employees wanted free wine too. They saw how special the DWP employees were treated, and demanded that a private RTD foundation be established. They had heard the steaks at the local fancy restaurants were filet mignon and imported from Argentina.

Mayor Cipitio found out about the DWP creative manner of raising funds and he was livid. He went into a violent rage and ordered his chief of staff to meet with the CEO of DWP at the Placita Olvera. He ordered that every Angeleno receive a free steak at Taix Restaurant.

The lines were massive. People lined up 4:00 a.m. to get in for dinner. Mayor Cipitio was a visionary. He already thought about reelection time. He figured that if he kept the masses well fed, they would vote for him again. He was a master planner.

He met with the heads of the different gangs in Los Angeles and offered them deals they could not refuse. First, he demanded they learn how to read and write English properly. He required they read all of Shakespeare's plays. Then, they had to divide the city into territories, with one catch: Mayor Cipitio took a five percent cut from every drug sale. He created the El Cipitio Foundation to give scholarships to the poorest kids in Los Angeles.

The Lakers were not doing enough to eradicate poverty. Mayor Cipitio asked his education policy director named Mr. Truant to design a program that reduced the dropout rate by ten percent in the first year. The Foundation offered full scholarships for every high school senior, and paid all university costs. Students could not believe it, especially the poor students whose parents were seamstresses, janitors, security guards, and substitute teachers. When the students graduated from colleges/universities they returned to their poor communities as doctors, lawyers, architects, and they rolled up their sleeves to help revitalized the area. They created small businesses that employed people from the community.

These students remembered how they had to go to bed hungry. Now they could give back through their education.

Students attended more regularly at Jordan, Manual Arts, Jefferson, Locke, Washington, and other schools that formerly had double-digit dropout rates. They talked about the best colleges or universities to apply to instead of the toughest gang or next ditching party. Racial animosity decreased. Race riots disappeared from local high schools and Latino and black student clubs worked together.

The El Cipitio Foundation had a major impact. Within one year hundreds of Los Angeles United School Districts (LAUSD) students applied and were accepted to the Ivy League universities. A ceremony was held at the Hollywood Bowl, where the thousands of scholarships were handed out to the students with their families. Mayor Cipitio created future voters for himself while doing something wonderful.

Students fantasized to be like Mayor Cipitio one day. Even though he was three feet tall, he was taller and more impressive than the Eiffel Tower.

Mayor Cipitio had created peace in the Middle East and Los Angeles, and now was known as the education mayor even though he never taught in a classroom, not even as a substitute teacher. Substitute teaching did not pay enough and no benefits were offered.

He based his experience on his street credibility and had visited many public schools. He hung out with teachers and gambled with them at MacArthur Park. Mayor Cipitio needed the extra cash and this offered him an opportunity to interact with the common folk, the gamblers, drug addicts, and teachers. He was proud of his grassroots approach. Mao's philosophy had rubbed off.

He founded a central committee—a group of five key advisors (who used code names: Big Fish, Mr. Greedy, Mr. Tabasco, Big Shark, and Mr. Developer) and or unofficial rulers of Los Angeles. He kept their names and identities secret. They were billionaires and owned the biggest businesses and land in Los Angeles. No one was supposed to know the identity of those on the central committee.

One of them was said to own the Lakers basketball team. The five individuals each had to pay the Chief of Police $100,000 per year, in a cash. They were given police badges and could do anything they wanted. No one knew the invisible men who controlled Los Angeles. Mayor Cipitio controlled them since he had files on each one of them, and they knew it.

Mayor Cipitio chose to be a kind and benevolent leader, but he was not stupid. The civil war, selling paletas, and his world travels had sharpened his insight and negotiating skills. He knew that evil men and women only understood deception, entrapment, and blackmail. They did not believe human beings could be trustworthy, loyal, and honest.

Their hearts were full of lizards, snakes, and poison. You could see the fog in their eyes and split tongues. Mayor Cipitio saw those signs when he met the evil people. He identified them easily since his dad represented that side of him.

Mayor Cipitio turned black at night, when he was evil and devious. During the day, he faded to white but his heart continued to be evil and wicked. He wished the color change was inverted, and have white mean evil and black mean good. He knew the United States was founded on racism, and certain men were not inherently equal before the law, like brown and black men. Mayor Cipitio's African roots had given him dark skin. He was proud of the fact.

His election as the first brown Mayor of Los Angeles was significant. He represented the oppressed and marginalized.

He was the future of Latin American leaders. Fidel Castro had set the example, but he was not truly indigenous.

Mayor Cipitio had broken so many barriers as an indigenous young man. He did not deny his Mayan and African roots and requested that Mayans perform at his events. He paid them $10,000 for each performance. He believed in paying fair wages to artists.

He helped other indigenous people move higher in the bureaucratic ranks. It was a first, not only for his own self-interest, but thousands of other indigenous and mestizo Latinos and African Americans. What an achievement. He was a confident leader. He did not fear other Latinos or African

Americans might tear him down or take his place. Mayor Cipitio overcame the colonized mentality.

His people had to confront that same mentality. He hated the crab syndrome, where one crab pulls down another instead of helping each other get out of the barrel. He wanted minorities to lift each other up instead of tearing each other down.

Mayor Cipitio called the President of the United States and requested a meeting. It was his first time with *El Presidente de Estados Unidos*. He flew coach instead of first class to show he was part of the common folk.

He was received with a red carpet at the Washington Dulles International Airport and local high school bands played while he descended from the airplane. It was a scene out of a Hollywood movie. Pandemonium broke out. Washington had never received a city mayor with so much enthusiasm. He created so much excitement that he was more popular than the President.

He distributed candies to everyone. Over a million people turned out from all ethnicities, races, and classes. No one had ever united the masses in such a manner.

The President met with Mayor Cipitio at a local coffee shop in the Adams Morgan neighborhood. They cut a deal, and the President gave him $10 billion to start a job creation program. The only condition was that Mayor Cipitio had to support him when he ran for reelection. He agreed. Of course, El Cipitio threw in a gift. He sent two high priced call girls to the Presidential suite where the Presidente was staying. They disguised themselves as cleaning ladies. They rocked the President's world all night long.

Mayor Cipitio came back a hero. He had a giant check made out to the City of Los Angeles. Hundreds of thousands of jobs were created with the $10 billion responsibly spent over a five-year period, no strings attached. The funding allowed the Mayor to hire and fire whoever he pleased since he controlled of the money. The Department of Labor and Department of Housing and Urban Development (HUD) signed official memos designating the funds as unrestricted.

He had a state of the art building constructed in South

Central Los Angeles where one hundred thousand jobs were created. The building and effort costs one billion dollars. He chose nine other areas (Boyle Heights, Rosemead, Culver City, San Pedro, Sun Valley, Koreatown, Crenshaw, Wilmington, and City of Terrace) to do the same. Each created one hundred thousand jobs, making one million jobs all together. His economic advisor made sure the new jobholders were supporters of Mayor Cipitio, establishing a lock in his reelection campaign.

With his innovative projects, Mayor Cipitio had more time to spend with the masses. He walked streets of poor neighborhoods and saw how the poor had to suffer the worst of companies that polluted and created health-related diseases from water and air contamination.

The state assembly members and senators were already bought off and they donated $5,000 to every nonprofit environmental organization to keep them from complaining about the problems.

He was granted a meeting with the Secretary of the Environmental Protection Agency (EPA), Mr. Benzine, through his close relationship with the President. They had solidified their friendship when they secretly attended a strip club in D.C.

To clean the environmental contamination from the poor neighborhoods, Mayor Cipitio asked for $20 billion from the EPA. He was serious. He threatened to publicly denounce the President for his complicity in allowing the companies to operate unregulated. He also had sex tapes on the President when he participated in a threesome with two cleaning ladies at the Hyatt Regency Hotel in Washington D.C.

Mayor Cipitio also stated that if he did not receive the $20 billion, he planned a protest march of over one million people. Imagine the total chaos when traffic came to a halt and federal employees did not show up for work, especially the EPA bureaucrats. The advice given to him by Reverend Al Sharpton came in handy.

The President had to give Mayor Cipitio the money. For the first time, companies cleaned up their pollution and implemented the use of green-friendly equipment. Green energy became big business. Also, the President told El Cipitio "give me back the original sex tapes and now we are even." El Cipitio agreed and now the President could sleep at night.

The major international environmental groups banded together and gave Mayor Cipitio a lifetime achievement award for his work. They called him "The Green Mayor." He laughed because he knew they just saw him as a little brown beaner.

One environmental group wanted to give Mayor Cipitio the Torta Award. They had assumed he was of Mexican descent. They should have called it the Pupusa Award, but the stuffing in a pupusa might not have been organic. The committee rescinded his nomination for the award and claimed that a greener candidate had emerged.

The truth was they had already purchased the Torta Award crystal and felt that the $100 investment was too much to cancel. They had retained the musical talent of Juan Gabriel to sing while the award was presented. The deposit for his performance had already been paid.

The event took place at Pasadena City College (PCC). Since the venue was free, over 10,000 students were expected to participate. However, the event was cancelled after complaints that the title was inappropriate and it should called the Hamburger or Hotdog Award. The oldest and largest Latino non-profit in Pasadena also threatened to boycott the event. It was easy to placate them, the President of PCC gave $500 to the non-profit. To shut them up. The Hispanic American advisors to the PCC President were pleased. They met at the Rose Tree Cottage to celebrate the ingenuity of the PCC President. They ordered Rose Petals hot tea and wore cotton white gloves.

The college administration said the change should follow the American tradition of football and baseball spirit.

Since Juan Gabriel was performing, the event moved to the Rose Bowl. Juan Gabriel wanted the Rose Bowl sprayed with odor of natural roses since the land where the Rose Bowl was built originally served as a garbage dump. The smell was intense.

One thousand gallons of rose spray were flown in, made out of imported roses from different countries.

The event was magnificent, with the mayor, councilmembers, and other dignitaries attending. They were so moved they gave out free cotton candy, which helped in their upcoming elections. Keeping the visitors and voters happy was very important. The image of the City of Roses could not be blemished.

It had to smell like roses. Anyone talking about the inequalities and injustices disappeared. They ended up under the Rose Bowl, similar to what dictator Mobutu Sese Seko did to political dissidents in Zaire, Africa when Muhammad Ali fought George Foreman. While the celebrations – tortures took place in private locker rooms of the Rose Bowl. The bodies of the tortured were buried along the San Gabriel Mountains.

Patrice Lumumba types of leaders were not allowed. Democracy was an illusion.

Mayor Cipitio studied the qualities and techniques used by Mobutu Seko and Lumumba. He leaned toward Lumumba since Mobutu was anti-communist.

He knew his murder was next. Since he was part of the undead, he could come back with vengeance, without mercy. The motherfucker was worse than a vampire.

Mayor Cipitio still wanted to do good and battled his inner demons. He tried to reject El Cadejo's blood but he could not.

He wanted to be more like La Siguanaba before she went crazy. She was the most compassionate woman in the world and a pioneer in women's rights, but he resent her drowning his ass on purpose.

Mayor Cipitio had restructured and improved the City of Los Angeles. He bridged the gap between the rich and poor, and created a thriving middle class. He provided opportunities for all students, regardless of their economic background or race.

He wanted a local political revolution. Chairman Mao inspired him to keep going every day. He did not want to be a martyr or tyrant, but sometimes he had to rule with an iron fist. He did not take shit from no one.

Mayor Cipitio had dedicated his life to selling paletas and now he sold dreams. He did pro bono work at the local drug rehabilitation center, and served as a therapist/counselor to former gang members and male and female prostitutes. Sometimes he provided advice while a little high on weed and getting over some wine tasting. He helped them because they were his confidants and advisors when he lived homeless on the streets. They shared newspapers to sleep on and packaged soups. His favorite was shrimp Cup O' Noodles. He said, "This shit is good," while reading *La Opinion* newspaper.

CHAPTER 10

HIS FIRST TERM OF OFFICE WENT SMOOTHLY. HOWEVER, Mayor Cipitio's reelection campaign turned very dirty. The chief of the LAPD had tapes of the mayor participating in wild Hollywood orgies. He did not give a fuck. He liked how he had performed and conducted himself in the videos. He was proud of not using bad words.

The videos boosted his popularity and motivated the less likely to vote be interested. They said, "He is one of us." People were also impressed with the rumor that his penis was extraordinarily huge. It was just a rumor and never confirmed. However, Stan Lee had taken a peak when El Cipitio was urinating. He even invited him to the show Super Humans but El Cipitio refused to participate. Stan Lee wanted El Cipitio to pull a giant truck, full of brand news cars, with his penis.

As the rumor grew, the campaign did not realize how much it helped. Talk shows focused on his penis size instead of important policy issues. Commentators took sides and said, "If we elect a mayor with a small penis, he will be insecure. We cannot go wrong with Mayor Cipitio."

He won the reelection easily. His opponents were crushed.

Mayor Cipitio ran his second term on cruise control and cut a few corners. He ordered the LAPD and LA Fire Department to hire his gangster friends without background checks.

The gangsters loved him for that. He gave them badges, guns, bullets, and power by using taxpayer money. Mayor Cipitio had inadvertently created his own personal army.

They walked around LA quoting *Scarface*, their ultimate hero. The new cops and firemen showed off their guns and high-powered rifles while mimicking Al Pacino: "Say hello to my little friend."

No mayor had created so many jobs, freeways, and metro rail stations. Mayor Cipitio had one billion trees planted, decreased the crime rate to almost zero, built many public schools, created new park space, and reversed the drop-out rates. He achieved so much that he began to get restless.

He considered whether to continue in politics or quit. He had options: run for US Senate, Governor, or just jump to President. He thought about the possibilities. He had to weigh his options.

How about a lobbyist or CEO of a major corporation? Any decision depended on what perks were offered. President of a university did not sound like a bad idea. Mayor Cipitio thought he was the perfect candidate to serve as token president of a community college. He could get away with doing very little work at certain community colleges since most boards of trustees did not hold the president accountable, especially those recovering from previously bad presidents. Even an incompetent president was kept until he or she retired. It was easier to keep a puppet on payroll since the professors and adjunct professors did all the heavy lifting anyway. The administrators continued to seek more funding to pay their own hefty salaries.

"Higher education is big business," said Mayor Cipitio. Its intent was to get students in debt, while the endowments of various universities continued to rise.

He knew the power brokers that ran the United States never really had to work since they had inherited their wealth in the billions. The accumulation started when they stole land from Native Americans and enslaved Blacks for forced labor. When Native Americans complained, they were placed on reservations. In the U.S. Constitution, minorities were not afforded basic rights. In Article I and Section 2 of the U.S. Constitution it states "Representatives and direct Taxes shall be apportioned among the several State which may be included within this Union, according to their respective Numbers, which shall be determined by adding to the whole Number of free Persons, including those bound to Service for a Term of Years, and excluding Indians not taxed, three fifths of all other Persons."

Mayor Cipitio knew the playing field was never level. It had been rigged since the 1500s, when the British, French, Spaniards, and other colonizers came to the Americas. Mayor Cipitio agreed with Malcolm X: The Pilgrims did not discover America; they used Plymouth Rock to beat the hell out of the Native Americans. Those who resisted were murdered.

His father, El Cadejo, had employed the same tactics in Central America: search, destroy, and control.

Mayor Cipitio had dreams of being embraced and accepted by his mother, that she never drowned him, and nurtured and took care of him. He imagined her carrying him in her arms, caressing his hair, providing milk from her voluptuous breast. But when he awoke, reality hit him like a ton of bricks.

He was angry, furious, enraged.

Running for US President was easy. His major international and local accomplishments gave him credibility as a serious contender.

The only problem was he needed an authentic birth certificate so he could claim he was born in the U.S. He rode a bus and got off on Alvarado to visit the Oaxacans and Guatemalans in MacArthur Park. They sold the best birth certificates. Obviously, he was not from the area. One man named Vicente asked, "*Que necesita compadre?*" and he said "*Pues que chingado—una pinche acta de nacimiento. Original.*" The man replied "*No hay pedo—solo cien bolas y se la tenemos mas tarde.*" Mayor Cipitio was in awe. This legitimate businessman simply provided a greatly needed service.

He gave him his full name, date of birth, and the hospital where he was born.

He returned later and the birth certificate was ready. He paid and even tipped him twenty dollars.

The birth certificate was amazing, printed on old paper with a seal of approval in purple ink. Those motherfuckers did not fuck around. They provided Mayor Cipitio with his ticket to the Presidency.

Mayor Cipitio needed to go *GQ* and shopped in high-end stores for tailored suits. He wanted the Tony Montana look. The tailors were impressed with Mayor Cipitio's confidence, attitude, and charisma.

They soon recognized him as the Mayor of the people. A guanaco tailor said, "*Me hizo soñar y creer que yo podia ser un tailor en* Beverly Hills." Mayor Cipitio nodded and told him "Whatever you need, just tell me."

That was one vote for the Presidency.

He loved white suits worn with a black vest. He wore shiny leather handmade imported Italian shoes. He was badder than John Travolta and Tony Montana. He wore a thick gold chain and did not give a fuck, and had Chairman Mao's little red book in his back pocket. Sometimes he carried the U.S. Constitution in case he was pulled over by the *chota*.

Mayor Cipitio stayed humble. He believed equality could be achieved if the rich distributed their wealth. One percent of society controlled most of the wealth. These were the bankers and corporate owners, the invisible men who really ran the United States.

He thought of duplicating his methods on the local level to the national level. Mao's attempt to industrialize China too fast had failed. Also, he initially encouraged his people to have as many children as they wanted. Mao quickly learned the limits of his country's resources.

Organizations like Slow-growth Parents pressured the Catholic Church to get Latinas to use birth control and not have children. The five white men known as The Riddler, The Penguin, The Joker, Mr. Freeze, Poison Ivy that ran the United States did not want the Latino/Hispanic population to grow too much, since one day a Latino progressive might be elected.

Mayor Cipitio made this one of his key campaign issues. Latina women should choose how many children they wanted, and he promised to provide the tools and resources for the children to obtain a quality education and a job once they graduated.

CHAPTER 11

MAYOR CIPITIO GREW CLOSER TO MAKING AN OFFICIAL decision about running for President. He recruited geniuses from high school dropouts, former felons, and a few Ph.D. candidates who were writing dissertations related to Presidential policy as his "Kitchen Cabinet." He also asked the Ph.D. candidates to conduct polling and demographic research.

His influences of Fidel Castro, Che Guevera, and Mao were paying off.

Fidel Castro showed him to learn a little bit of every subject to become an expert himself and how to avoid eating food poisoned by the CIA. Che Guevara showed him not to be stupid by trying to create an uprising in a country like Bolivia, where the population was not ready for such an effort. Mao showed him to slowly make progress in agriculture and technology, have a balance, not allow corporations to pollute the air and water, and control global warming.

Mayor Cipitio spent his evenings reading about the fall of the Aztec, Maya, and Inca empires. He analyzed the role natural disasters played and how diseases contributed in destroying whole generations.

Infighting had contributed in bringing down these great empires. He knew traitors emerged.

Mayor Cipitio had to do everything in his power to prevent internal dissent and destruction. He had to resort to his El Cadejo side and disappear any traitors. He did not like Stalin but he knew that one of his gifts was brutality. He had risen to power by murdering his competition.

Mayor Cipitio did not want what happened to Che Guevara happen to him.

He learned from people like Nixon to follow and record every move made by his closest advisors and enemies. Phones were tapped, computers were hacked, and secret video surveillance placed in every office, living room, and bedroom that were involved in his campaign. He received weekly summary reports.

He wanted to know the weaknesses of each enemy and closest ally. If his economic advisor had an addiction to weed, he wanted to know. If his secretary was having an affair, he wanted to know. He practiced the motto, "Knowledge is power."

Mayor Cipitio became omnipresent, like Jesus Christ.

He adjusted his personality depending on the audience.

With young people, he used "fuck," "bitch," and "shit" in every other sentence to keep it real. He acted careless like their heroes too, with an attitude of not giving a fuck, letting his pants sag at times. One of his heroes was the Mexican comedian/actor Cantinflas and he got the idea to sag his pants from Cantinflas. El Cipitio farted, burped, and talked shit in front of teenagers. They were in awe that such a little fucker had the audacity to act like them. Mayor Cipitio knew their psyche since he was truly ten years old, but with an old soul.

When addressing the Chamber of Commerce, he spoke MBA lingo and dropped certain words or names of business owners to appear chummy with the business elite. He wanted their trust. He wore tuxedos to the events and sprayed on his cigar cologne. The businesspeople loved how he walked around a room, sipped wine with a smile, and shook hands firmly.

He looked deep into their eyes with confidence. They loved him. He was supportive of big, giant projects like building an underground metro that went from Los Angeles to New York, Boston, and Miami. The price tag was not a barrier.

The only issue he had to think about was the building of a

giant underground oil pipeline. He was undecided because he needed the donations from big business.

He spoke with his environmental advisor, Mr. TreeHugger who happened to be executive director of the Sierra Club. Mayor Cipitio had a choice to make: support his economic advisor—who happened to be president and CEO of the US Chamber of Commerce—or the director of the Sierra Club. Not an easy choice. The National Parks Conservative Association wanted to obtain the support from Mayor Cipitio. But he refused to do business with them since they did not speak Spanish. Some of their members only spoke Shakespearean English. El Cipitio was especially offended when NPCA wanted to give him the *green enchilada award.*

He set up steak dinner meetings at Taix to broker deals and stall as much as possible. The wine never stop pouring and people stuff themselves while children were going hungry in the surrounding ghetto neighborhoods.

The day came. Mayor Cipitio was running for President and he had to select an appropriate location. It had to be powerful and symbolic. He settled on the Statue of Liberty to symbolize the positive contributions immigrants had made in helping build America.

He asked his kitchen cabinet to write a monumental speech for him, and for his Ph.D. candidate volunteers to recruit organizers from Cal Berkeley and other universities, especially those supportive in weed being smoked on campus to help with creativity and human tolerance.

His goal was to get one million individuals to join him on Liberty Island. He wanted representatives of every layer of society to attend and participate, and eventually become his base of supporters and volunteers. He offered free tacos, pupusas, hamburgers, and hot dogs. He wanted to be inclusive.

He had big dilemma. The big alcohol companies wanted to sponsor the event. They each gave him $1 million to promote their brands, and provided free beer to the masses. El Cipitio had to talk it over with his kitchen cabinet. They met at the Beer Factory Restaurant.

Initially they had reservations, but the brewers sent models representing Corona, Negra Modelo, Budweiser, Heineken, and other brands. The models were stunning. Each served beer. After downing over ten beers each, the kitchen cabinet changed their minds.

They agreed after downing twenty beers each, and said, "Hell yes, we will do it," "Fuck yeah," and "*Que viva la revolucion*," once they reached thirty beers each. The kitchen cabinet became so bold they asked for chicken wings, sushi, and egg rolls to be included with the free beer. It had to be multicultural.

El Cipitio was persuaded. His El Cadejo side overruled his ethics. El Cipitio had to announce that he would not run for a Mayoral reelection. He began to plan to run for *Presidente* of the United States of America. He had to set up a team that would help him get the Presidential nomination at the Democratic National Convention.

He had to hide his insatiable need for beer and weed. The AK-47 bullet that went through his brain caused constant migraines. During his time in the Middle East, doctors recommended he smoke weed to alleviate his headaches.

He had so much stress that the Jews and Palestinians got him to drink a lot of beer just to go to sleep. He smoked weed when he negotiated peace. Man, did Bob Marley's "I am Rebel" impress him. He played the song in the background while they drank beer and smoked weed.

That was his secret weapon. Anytime he wanted to influence others, he played Bob Marley.

El Cipitio needed a book describing his achievements, adventures, and exploits. He searched for an Ivy League professor to write his biography. He asked Cornel West to write it and he agreed. Cornel "Of course, my brother in the struggle."

Starship's song, "Nothing's Gonna Stop Us Now," opened his announcement that he was running for President. You could hear the song throughout New York and New Jersey.

The masses were inspired. Chairman Mao would have been proud.

El Cipitio had made the Great Leap Forward, and he liked it.

He travelled to every state of the Union and met people from all backgrounds: rural, urban, poor, middle class, and rich. He listened to their dreams and aspirations, and their needs.

He learned how to listen when he was a *paletero*. He listened to people's problems and better than any psychotherapist or psychiatrist. People felt as if they were the most important person in the world when they spoke to El Cipitio. He had more true empathy than a monk who had practiced yoga all his life.

El Cipitio had inner wisdom, patience, superior knowledge, and most importantly, he had mastered his emotions. It did not matter where he was. He could be serene even during a hurricane. People tested him. At rallies, various people cursed him out: "You motherfucking shorty piece of shit, I'll fuck you up. I don't give a fuck that you are running for President. Motherfucker *frijolero*."

He smiled and walked away. He practiced Gandhi's philosophy of nonviolent resistance. But deep inside he wanted to fuck them up, cut them into pieces, and eat them as *sopa de res* or *sopa de pata*.

He impressed voters in Iowa, Minnesota, and tougher states such as Kentucky, Alabama, and Georgia, where Ku Klux Klan (KKK) members showed up to observe the little fucker running for President. They wanted to kill him until they heard him speak—they were mesmerized. He spoke like a racist Southerner and appealed to their deepest long-held political views.

He promised federal subsidies for farmers, free water, more food stamps, bigger welfare checks, and free tickets to rodeos, arm-wrestling contests, and gator-hunting competitions. El Cipitio was so fucking devious that he promised them new high-tech trailers with free air conditioning. That sealed the deal.

The little fucker was unstoppable. He promised everyone what they really wanted and appealed to their secret dreams. The South had a kinship with Aztec and Mayan people, as some had settled in the Blue Ridge Mountains. Their temples and ruins have never been discovered.

One rumor had a civilization of Aztecs and Mayans existing underground, with secret tunnels that led to Southern Mexico and Central America. No wonder the flow of immigration never stopped.

The farmers were thrilled when they met with El Cipitio. He wore overalls and knew more about farming than they did. He gave tips on how grow faster and bigger corn, and taught them secrets of the Mayans. But he asked for favors in return: to support him and get all of their friends to vote for him. El Cipitio's campaign slogan was "El Cipitio—Salt of the Earth—One of Us." He also promised that once elected, Willie Nelson would come and perform.

Commercials showed the farmers at a picnic with El Cipitio, eating jam, beans, and drinking local beer—they provided the grain for the beer companies. The farmers wanted assurance from El Cipitio they could get the national/international contracts to sell more grain for beer production. The candidate said, "Yes, I am one of you."

El Cipitio's favorite part of the campaign was in New York and Florida. The Puerto Rican parade in New York named him Grand Marshall. Dominicans loved him because he almost looked like them. Going to Florida meant hanging out with the Cubans. He loved their beans and music, and was the big hit at their celebrations. El Cipitio imitated their accents and the loved it since they saw it as cute. That little fucker was so sneaky he got the attention and support from Celia Cruz. She agreed to make a song for him, and she called it *"Azucar—Mi Cipitio Tiene Tumbao."* El Cipitio affectionately called her *"Mami."*

When El Ciptio appeared on "Don Francisco Presenta," he wore Huggies diapers to make his butt stick out. The audience went crazy when Celia Cruz joined him and sang "Azucar—Mi Cipitio Tiene Tumbao." Univision had the highest ratings in their history. That night El Cipitio and Celia Cruz rode together in their limosine and spent some quiet time together. He felt motherly love coming from Celia and his heart was filled with joy.

They beat every major network throughout the United

States and world. The episode became an international phenomenon. El Ciptio was ahead of his time—as usual. The audience was mesmerized by how he shook his ass with such precision, glamour, and eroticism.

He gained millions of new followers and supporters. *Playboy* considered having El Cipitio as the first male to appear on the cover.

His campaign headquarters received millions of fan letters and campaign contributions. Many of the checks and money orders were for only one dollar, but he managed to raise over a one hundred million dollars with the small contributions.

With his campaign song, "Nothing's Gonna Stop Us Now," *Dance World* invited El Cipitio to participate. He was a big hit when he danced to the song on live television, making moves that were extraordinary. The Black community adored him. He visited Harlem, South Central Los Angeles, and Philadelphia. He spent not just one day with them, but two or three. He adopted their styles and manner of speaking. These came naturally to him since he had lived with the Black community for many years when he was selling paletas.

Prince and Quincy Jones decided to support him and they played a fundraising concert to benefit El Cipitio at The Apollo. Prince sang the classic "Superfreak" for El Cipitio, and introduced the song with, "This is for the short motherfucker who is really freaky."

The only community El Cipitio had having a hard time reaching was the Asian community. He had never interacted with them, except occasionally eating at Yoshinoya. He told his friends they had the best Chinese food. When he went to a Korean restaurant, he ordered sushi. He also cracked politically incorrect jokes that offended the Asians. When he visited the Indianapolis 500 races, he made an off-hand remark, "Where the Asian race car drivers?"

He said he was trying to be funny. El Cipitio had to apologize to every Asian civil rights organization in the United States.

Capturing that community's support and vote was an uphill battle. He became so desperate that he appeared at rallies dressed as Ultraman. They laughed at him.

He asked his kitchen cabinet for suggestions and ideas. Mr. Ford said he should buy a Toyota, and he did. Support came in from Japanese American businessmen. He ate at local Korean restaurants and became obsessed with Korean BBQ ribs. The Koreans liked him because he participated in Karaoke competitions. El Cipitio became proficient to the point where he was invited to participate in a Korean karaoke competition. He was great at imitating Elvis Presley. He loved singing Elvis songs, especially "Burning Love."

He watched tapes of Elvis performances at night and practiced his every move. He requested a tailored leather "American Eagle" jumpsuit like the white one Elvis wore for his *Aloha from Hawaii* performances, only he asked for his in black.

El Cipitio blew everyone away at the karaoke competition. He was the best. The Korean American community went bananas. They loved him so much they gave him awards.

The Chinese American community from San Marino, Arcadia, and San Gabriel, noticed El Cipitio's fame in the Japanese and Korean communities. They asked, "What about us?"

El Cipitio had a secret he could not reveal to them, that his hero and mentor was Chairman Mao. He had to be creative. He was finally invited to the San Gabriel Chinese Parade.

Instead of riding in a car, El Cipitio walked the parade route as one of the men in the dragon dance. He was a hit. The crowd could not believe the short man could move and swing the head of the dragon in such a furious manner. El Cipitio ordered special fireworks from China. These were illegal, but he used connections with the Chinese underworld.

The fireworks he used in his dragon performance had colors were so amazing that he made the front page of the *World Journal* Chinese-language newspaper. The headline read: "El Cipitio—Honorary Chinese." He spent more time in LA's Chinatown, where he brokered deals for the Chinese mob to sell illegal weapons to the KKK.

He was a fucking genius. He banked with the China Trust Bank and joined the San Marino Chamber of Commerce.

Donations started to roll in. He hired protection from the Chinese mob. He promised that at least one, possibly two, would serve in his Presidential security team as bodyguards.

They promised him access to the Chinese government in case he needed favors.

Now he had support from various Asian communities. The Southeast Asian communities slowly followed. El Cipitio became in awe of Buddhism. He began to connect with his body, mind, and soul. He wanted his heart to remain healthy. He wanted to achieve balance in his life – he did not want to become sick like Franklin Delano Roosevelt.

The petroleum industry, pharmaceutical, tobacco, air and space technology, manufacturing, banking, and many other special interest groups courted El Cipitio.

He asked his kitchen cabinet to meet with them and provide a one-page summary from each meeting that included a dollar amount donation.

When in public, he denounced those companies as out of control, greedy, and profit mongering. He painted them as the devil; they reminded him of his father, El Cadejo.

He confided with friends, Mr. Ethics, Mr. Morality, and Mr. Straight Arrow that the special interest groups had no moral compass, compassion, or ethics. They were all about the bottom line, making profits and buying people, and contributing to the murder of thousands of civilians while they counted stupendous profits.

The CEOs and lobbyists flew on private jets. They owned islands and ate organic food from Whole Foods. They invited El Cipitio to visit their extravagant mansions, but he refused. He was a man of the people, like Chairman Mao.

El Cipitio adopted a strict diet. He wanted to be slimmer so he could withstand the demands of the White House. He imagined himself in the White House as the first mestizo/ indigenous President. He kept his African roots quiet.

But something was missing: La Cholita. He could impress her as a serious presidential contender. He figured to convince her he was a badass boy.

He thought about his unprecedented power as Commander-in-Chief, and the legal power to order sanctioned murders under the disguise of national security. El Cipitio saw himself become *el jefe, El mero mero.*

He asked his kitchen cabinet to find La Cholita.

With her as his soul mate at the White House, they would have uninterrupted sex in the White House bedroom on a $10,000 orthopedic Luv bed, handmade for kings and queens.

La Cholita was found doing time an all-women's prison for drug smuggling, but she had only been dealing weed.

El Cipitio went to the prison undercover. He used a different identification the Chinese got for him; they had infiltrated the Department of Motor Vehicles (DMV) on Rosemead Boulevard and printed any identification they pleased.

Seeing La Cholita again excited the little man. He made one last attempt to convince her to leave her wicked, illegal ways. He told her about his evil side so she knew he was badass bad boy, a very bad boy that ate people. An official mobster.

He had joined the most elite mob in the world with the most sophisticated weapons, and legally allowed to get rid of people. Of course, many were secret operations.

La Cholita was glad to see him but he fit the profile of a goody two-shoes and she wanted a biker dude living on the edge with black biker boots. She used to go for the cholo look but she wanted more diversity.

She fantasized about leather and loved its smell.

El Cipitio was moved to see her. She was fine as hell.

They talked and held hands. She promised to think about being with him, but she had mental health issues he needed to be aware of. La Cholita admitted her addiction to prescribed medication. She had quit weed and alcohol to end up hooked on legal drugs. She could not stand being alone and she confided in El Cipitio by telling him "drugs fill the deep hole in soul and they numb my pain from the past."

She had multiple personalities, panic attacks, and a mild form of schizophrenia. El Cipitio did not give a fuck. Once he became President, the Surgeon General would be the private physician for his future wife.

CHAPTER 12

EL CIPITIO BELIEVED HE COULD DO ANYTHING, AND TO anyone. He was addicted to power, deal making, and being in the spotlight. He figured that he could get away with anything, especially as President.

The FBI should sweep his office once a week to get rid of bugs, and search and destroy any bugs in his home.

El Cipitio was paranoid. His experiences from the civil war in Central America had left him with Post Traumatic Stress Disorder (PTSD) and certain words, sounds, smells, and people reminded him of what had happened. He was angry, depressed, and reclusive.

His kitchen cabinet was aware of his condition. They had to keep any mental problems secret, or risk seeing El Cipitio discredited like Michael Dukakis when he ran for President in 1988. Dukakis had seen a psychiatrist and the Bush campaign managers made sure the information became public. Among the voting population, going to see a psychiatrist meant he was major crazy.

El Cipitio kept his PTSD a secret. He considered taking medication but he was afraid of being dependent.

He drank beer to relax and control his nerves.

In the final stretch of the campaign, his opponents attacked him as too young, too short, and inexperienced.

He agreed to one national debate with all the candidates. El

Cipitio had become the frontrunner and the other candidates decided to join forces for merciless attack on him.

Stories circulated that El Cipitio was a drug addict, womanizer, and member of the mob. These were based on stereotypes from television. Some people believed the rumors and his kitchen cabinet recommended an interview by Charlie Rose.

He agreed. Charlie Rose stayed up the night before to prepare and had to take a two-hour nap before interviewing El Cipitio. This promised to be one of his toughest interviews. Charlie planned to confront El Cipitio with medical records obtained from an informant. The PTSD diagnosis was going public.

Announcements for the interview made it sound like a World Wrestling Federation royal rumble, bigger than a match between Andre the Giant versus Hulk Hogan. The question was, who would win Charlie Rose or El Cipitio?

Charlie had rarely interviewed such an interesting character. Deep in his coat pocket was more information about El Cipitio not even his colleagues knew about. He had questions he did not write down since he was afraid someone might find out.

The day finally arrived. El Cipitio dressed properly; he had personally ironed his clothes. He chose not to wear a tie since he wanted to project an image of the man of the people. He wore jeans.

He wanted to show Charlie who was boss.

Charlie met him in the green room and could not believe El Cipitio was only three feet tall. He almost laughed and struggled with his composure. El Cipitio gave him his death-squad look. Charlie backed down.

The interview began on stage at the round table. The first questions were soft as Charlie warmed up.

After fifteen minutes of small talk, Charlie dropped his bomb. He asked, "Are you in fact suffering from STD?" El Cipitio was offended. "What the fuck are you talking about"? Charlie fumbled and dropped the cards with the rest of his questions for the first time. They were mixed up.

Charlie said, "I meant PTSD, post-traumatic stress disorder, not STD. That's short for Sexually Transmitted Disease." El

Cipitio said, "Thank you for the correction, Mr. Rose. Any document supporting your allegation is a breach of doctor-patient privacy. I will sue my psychiatrist and the Betty Ford Center as soon as I talk with my lawyer." He was furious but remained calm and collected. He projected the Godfather attitude; El Cipitio was so sneaky he had cotton on his cheeks so he could talk like Marlon Brando.

El Cipitio admitted to having PTSD but that it not exclude him from running for President. He said he had bigger issues and revealed secrets about his three opponents. One was involved in attempted murder, a drive-by shooting; the second had been caught pissing in front of a preschool and now a registered sex offender; and the third had an affair with Richard Nixon.

Charlie's jaw dropped.

Now El Cipitio was on the offensive. He questioned Charlie and his lack of inclusion and diversity in the *Charlie Rose Show*. El Cipitio asked him why, except for a few token minorities, he only invited rich white guests.

Charlie almost walked out of the interview, but he chose to defend his integrity. He said Oprah was a close friend and he had many dark-skinned friends. None of his neighbors were dark but he sat next to minorities at the local Red Lobster Restaurant.

In the last five minutes, Charlie said he had a final question. "Are you gay, Mr. Cipitio?"

El Cipitio started to laugh and said the only gay encounter he had was when he play dick swords with his friends in kindergarten and first grade, and based on innocence and curiosity. El Cipitio handled the response masterfully.

Charlie had no more ammunition and he simply said, "Good luck, Mr. Cipitio."

El Cipitio jumped off the seat and walked out. His last words to Charlie as he exited were "Fuck you, bitch." This encounter helped for Charlie Rose to become a household name. Many kids on playgrounds started saying "don't be a little bitch like Charlie Rose." El Cipitio inspired children throughout the world to stand up and walk away when being mistreated.

The producers were impressed with the little fucker. He bowed to no one and the ratings were off the charts. The sympathy toward El Cipitio became tremendous and the lesbian, gay, bisexual, and transgender (LGBT) community defended him. He became their poster child. When asked if he supported same sex marriage, El Cipitio said, "Hell yeah."

The LGBT community was so impressed with the little fucker they donated millions of dollars. He met privately with their leadership and promised them a post on the U.S. Supreme Court and another as Secretary of Defense.

El Cipitio had one more month to campaign. The countdown was on.

He visited every single state, city, and small farmlands. He went to Alaska to meet with the Eskimos.

During the last days of campaigning, he chose to do a fast for two days in support of Native American rights. He made his point by sleeping in a reservation high in the mountains of New Mexico. El Cipitio broke his fast at one of the best restaurants in Albuquerque with steak, beans, and chile. He signed autographs and praised the mixture of Mexican, Native American, and Spanish food in New Mexico. He locked up support from that state.

No one cared about his candidate for Vice President Mr. Who since El Cipitio had become a household name. Millions of households had a black and white headshot photograph of El Cipitio in their living room. He was seen as a family member.

Election Day had the highest turnout ever in the United States. El Cipitio invited observers from other countries to be sure no fraud occurred.

The NBC, CBS, and ABC networks ran live coverage.

They had never seen so much excitement, not even for John F. Kennedy.

The lines to vote were tremendous, and some extended for miles. People wore tee shirts with the face of El Cipitio and the slogans "We are One" or "We are Family."

At seven o'clock in the evening, the polls officially closed and the count began.

Seven hours later, seventy percent of the polls were counted and El Cipitio was in first place.

The campaign started to celebrate. At eight o'clock the following morning, it was official — El Cipitio had won.

He was in awe when he learned that he was the President-elect. Then a miracle occurred: La Cholita called. "I want to join you," she said. "I want to be your partner and your backbone."

El Cipitio was ecstatic. Being President-elect influenced others in unimaginable ways.

He invited La Cholita to the inauguration.

She said she did not want to get married but they could shack up. He agreed.

Finally, he had scored with La Cholita. The media spread the word El Cipitio was not officially married and the barbed tongues in the nation's capital started wagging.

Pope Heresy said he saw no problem with the President-elect not being married, and sent a letter of approval to El Cipitio. The Pope was smart; he wanted stronger relations with the United States and the letter was his olive branch.

Anytime anyone complained, El Cipitio showed the Pope's letter.

The letter soon appeared on the front pages of every major newspaper. It was so eloquently written, no spelling or grammatical errors. The media was in awe of the poetry the Pope had written, and impressed by his command of English. They were not aware he had obtained his Ph.D. in divinity at England's Oxford University.

The Pope asked El Cipitio if he could attend the inauguration and help with the planning details. El Cipitio said yes.

The ceremony was majestic. La Cholita dressed in black satin and looked splendid. El Cipitio wore an elegant black suit.

He wrote his speech at the Coffee Bean in North Hollywood while he ate a yogurt. The contents of the speech was amazing. It was on par with Abraham Lincoln's Emancipation Declaration. He mesmerized the two million people that attended the swearing-in ceremony in Washington D.C.

Over two hundred presidents, prime ministers, kings, and

queens attended. It was the biggest turnout of heads of state. The men wanted to see La Cholita dressed in satin. She had the magical power to give them an orgasm when near her or a double orgasm by shaking their hand.

They also wanted to see the sheer lingerie she wore for the ceremony. The Pope had to keep his eyes above her waist. During the ceremony, the Pope had an orgasm without touching anyone for the first time. He prayed deeply. He felt like a true sinner.

The Pope did not judge La Cholita because part of his family had been part of a human smuggling operation, and the women forced to work as strippers. Of course, he never supported such illegal actions.

He was a man of the cloth. His faith had elevated him to the highest position of the Catholic Church. He was also a non-judgmental pope. He accepted everyone, even the little fucker that stood three feet tall and could blast your ass in a second. The Pope confided to his closest advisors that El Cipitio was an upstanding citizen and that no one should judge him since everyone sins.

Now the little fucker had access to missiles. Nobody wanted to fuck with him. Stories of his violent past started swirling around but it was kept hush, hush. He became like that kid in the *Twilight Zone* episode, "It's a Good Life," where Bill Mumy could read people's minds and if they had bad thoughts, he disappeared them.

President Cipitio pardoned certain individuals. Fans of Simon & Garfunkel were required to sing "The Sound of Silence." If they sang with passion, he gave them a second chance. They liked him so much that Simon agreed to put his personal differences aside with Garfunkel. They would do this for El Cipitio. Only a El Cipitio could reunite duos and music bands that had already broken up.

The President thought Simon & Garfunkel were gay lovers, but he was just stereotyping since he was not used to seeing two men so close. They slept in the same bed on a single bed mattress when on tour. This closeness inspired them to be amazing musicians, with much emotion and sincerity. Of course, this revelation was made through *The Enquirer* tabloid.

President Cipitio was just relieved to have won the election and to be with La Cholita.

Now the real work began.

At his first official press conference, reporters asked if La Cholita spoke English or Spanglish, and if she was born here.

The President warned every reporter that if they continued with stupid questions, they would be placed on a black list and banned from attending briefings at the White House.

The reporters got the message and shifted their focus. They asked serious policy-related issues and who he planned to appoint to Cabinet positions.

President Cipitio wanted a Secretary of State and Secretary of Defense with zero tolerance toward generals and dictators that tortured and raped, or kidnapped children to be boy soldiers.

He knew how harsh it was to be trained, brainwashed, and forced to torture and kill his own people. He wanted to end those operations where children were destroyed.

President Cipitio promised to use his powers to punish those who deserved it, instead of innocent civilians.

He invested billions of dollars for education for youth and adults, and only countries that respected human rights received foreign aid. Leaders from developing countries also began to admire El Cipitio and they coined a nickname for him "El Cipitio tiene corazon."

Less money went to the Pentagon and more in creating better schools and paying teachers better salaries.

In China, teachers were seen as heroes, but not in the United States, which was a major contradiction.

He raised annual teacher salaries to $100,000 to start. His economic advisors set caps on how much corporate and banking CEOs could earn, similar to the sliding scale established for nonprofits by the Center for Nonprofit Management. The salaries had to be reined in.

More accountability was implemented toward banks

and corporations. They no longer had carte blanche with the politicians in Washington DC.

President Cipitio's base of support was so tremendous that he could win reelection with their small donations. The message was clear: he could not be bought off.

Finally, he was his own man. All he needed was La Cholita and his two balls.

He wore tee shirts printed with, "Say hello to my little two balls." He was irreverent in the White House and walked around like he fucking owned the place, and had built it with his own hands.

The European side of his father, El Cadejo, came out and gave President Cipitio a sense of superiority and entitlement. He acted like he owned the stock market too.

La Cholita changed her life: she studied foreign languages, took etiquette courses, and dressed in a very upscale, elegant manner.

The country became enamored with her, just like with Jackie Kennedy.

La Cholita had tea meetings at the White House, provided tours for the public, and gave one-on-one interviews with specific journalists. She gave interviews in English, Spanish, Armenian, and Arabic. She was gifted with languages.

Her family, who went by the last name Aztlan, did not like President Cipitio since he had guanaco blood. They were hardcore Mexican Americans who had worked in the fields alongside Cesar Chavez. They did not like recent immigrants and La Cholita's man represented the immigrant success story.

From *paletero* to President: they were jealous that he skipped centuries and won the presidency so easily.

For her family, he was El Mojado. They did not admire his qualities or that he had walked through Guatemala and Mexico to get to the United States. They referred to President Cipitio as "the lawbreaker." When La Cholita's mother and father saw him on television celebrating Memorial Day weekend — wearing a tee shirt with the U.S. flag — they were infuriated. They said, "Look at that illegal."

La Cholita made them promise not to give away the fact

that President Cipitio was undocumented and had bought his US citizen identity.

She gave them free trailer homes for them to remain quiet for the next four years. But soon they started blackmailing her, demanding free drugs. She had to find out how to get free drugs and became close friends of the wife, Ms. Mota, of the Drug Enforcement Agency (DEA) director Mr. Mota. He was proud that his wife was a cocktail party friend of La Cholita.

She showed La Cholita where her husband kept large amounts of confiscated drugs, in empty cargo boxes at the Long Beach port. La Cholita had a spare key so she could take a few pounds every once in a while for recreational purposes. She gave five pounds of each drug to her greedy parents.

The drugs kept them quiet and happy. Drugs took them to a place of refuge. A place where everything was just right. They could escape from reality.

President Cipitio had no clue that this was going on. He started a crusade as the anti-drug President. At major drug busts, he was invited for the discovery and burning of the shipments. He had zero tolerance for drug trafficking.

He wanted to be reelected without using drug money. Many paleteros had overdosed on the mean streets of South Central Los Angeles. No one cared about them since they were poor minorities, the invisible.

The President could change things for the better. He was still a dreamer.

Corrupt guerrillas and the military, Bolovia, Colombia, Nicaragua, Honduras, El Salvador, and Mexico helped each other transport drugs in Latin America. They did not care who became addicted or were murdered. The guerrillas and military even blew up bridges to sell the rebuilding contracts to foreign companies. They got big kickbacks for each bridge they destroyed.

Military officers transported guns, bombs, and ammunition and sold them to the guerrilla rebels. No wonder US aid was ineffective. The military used the money to buy more weapons, and resold them in the black market. The drug trade funded many guerrilla leaders. They also obtain money from Europe and the U.S. to build a superhighway connecting Central America with Colombia. Drug shipments were easily driven in trucks from Colombia, through Central America, into Mexico, and finally the US.

The government did nothing to stop those illegal activities. American drug cartels established businesses to do the import and exporting, and applied for loans from the Small Business Administration. They claimed to be minority owned but the true leaders of the American cartels lived in Texas in big mansions.

Some chose to invest in the distributing crack cocaine in South Central Los Angeles to raise money to fund the Nicaraguan Contras. Of course, they gave a little cut from the profits to the CIA agents, some law enforcement and FBI agents, and Voice of America State Department funded radio programs. They hated PBS television programming and did not give them one cent.

It was all corrupt.

CHAPTER 13

As COMMANDER IN CHIEF OF THE UNITED STATES, President Cipitio figured he could stop civilians from being murdered by creating highly trained death squads.

Only the President and General Ripper knew about the squads. They were deployed to various parts of the world, where they tortured and murdered their targets.

La Cholita knew nothing about the operations.

President Cipitio was so fucking busy putting hits on people around the world, he paid less attention to La Cholita. She felt lonely and depressed, and relied on prescribed medication to fill the void of her loneliness.

She longed for her past life, when she was anonymous and could smoke a joint any time. In the White House, she needed OxyContin and other pills to go to sleep.

Her beauty and sex appeal had remained. President Cipitio saw what was happening, and promised her the rod of love.

She caressed the President's big head. After a night of wild sex, they relaxed and fell asleep.

President Cipito developed a great idea after his orgasm.

Why not have the wealthiest corporations and banks donate part of their billions of dollars to send humanitarian aid to developing countries instead of selling them weapons?

He asked the Cabinet to set up a meeting with the wealthiest Americans. No one knew about the incredible list or had access to it. The wealthiest were so secretive they had established a secret society, the Elysiums.

They met at midnight in Pasadena, CA to plan their investments and manipulate the stock market. Members of the society informed each other where to invest. It was insider trading at the highest levels. No wonder they never lost their incredible wealth. It just kept growing.

President Cipitio had their attention when he walked in, along with the chairwoman of the Federal Reserve and director of Internal Revenue Service (IRS). He gave the society members an ultimatum: either voluntarily donate to social causes or the federal government would release information about their society and self-serving investments.

They were outraged but the wealthiest gentleman, Mr. Fatso said, "Cooler heads will prevail." He promised to donate $50 billion to get the ball rolling.

President Cipitio kissed both cheeks of the wealthiest man, imitating Don Corleone from *The Godfather*. The other men were impressed with the President's ways of persuasion.

He raised over one trillion dollars in one hour.

The Secretary of State and other members of his cabinet who were experts in foreign investment were called into the Oval Office. He sat with the owners of the world's biggest credit companies and set a cap on interest rates for loans to developing countries at seven percent.

It was a monumental task for his economic team. They had to figure out how to divide, invest, and set up protocol and policies.

Dictators had to conduct free elections if they wanted a piece of the action. They were hesitant but they agreed, otherwise President Cipitio might resort to his evil ways and send his death squads. They knew better than to fuck with the little man. He was tougher that Genghis Kahn and Napoleon put together. He was a fucking giant even though he stood three feet tall.

He had meetings with the organized crime leaders that ran some of the countries and told them they had to abide by his rules.

The President's economic team advised El Cipitio to invest $500 billion in Africa, $300 billion in Latin America, and $100 billion in Asia. The remaining $100 billion was for miscellaneous loans and gifts to various countries.

The money was spent in building schools and providing scholarships for individuals to attend universities to obtain their degrees and become full-time teachers. Technology hubs were created for training in different job trades and careers, and graduates went on to establish their own businesses and hired workers.

No money was invested in military or defense. Most countries were forced to demilitarize and commit to peace. The Generals who profited from selling weapons in the black market were outraged. But they knew that they could not betray or disrespect El Ciptio. They had to follow his orders. Otherwise, death was certain. El Cipitio was still more feared than loved.

The plan worked. President El Cipitio, the fucking little genius, had done it again.

The people in those countries no longer had to starve or work as slaves. Many became teachers, business owners, and proud workers who helped others. The countries thrived in an accelerated manner. Neither Kennedy's Alliance for Progress nor Lyndon Johnson's War on Poverty were as successful.

Everything was going well. President Cipitio was the most nonviolent President of the United States. He was a combination of great leaders in history, yet he was recognized as a legend and revered leader while living. He stood taller than his role model and inspiration, Chairman Mao. Mao had almost a billion followers.

President Cipitio had over five billion supporters around the world. Of course, there were the haters, but he did not give a fuck.

All he wanted was La Cholita. She rocked his world every night.

Soon his world became controversial.

El Cadejo immigrated to Los Angeles in search of his long lost son. La Siguanaba also moved to Los Angeles and underwent psychiatric treatment. She cleaned homes for a couple in Beverly Hills and they recommend the best shrinks. She told the psychiatrist about the terrible deed she had committed, that she had drowned her newborn child and gave away his twin. She felt relieved to be able to tell somebody.

El Cadejo looked in South Central for his son. His sixth sense told him he was still alive.

Soon, El Cadejo's world collided with La Siguanaba. He had obtained a job as a gardener in Beverly Hills, and ended up working at the same mansion as La Siguanaba.

By this time, they had taken English classes at the Belmont and Evans community adult schools. El Cadejo saw La Siguanaba, and was disrespectful and a true asshole. "Bitch, where is my son?"

She cried and told him that she had drowned his ass. El Cadejo was furious. His diabolic spirits had whispered to him that his son was alive.

La Siguanaba was ecstatic and could not believe it.

They submitted their DNA to the national database to find a match for their son.

When they received the results, they almost fainted.

The only person with the same DNA was none other than President Cipitio.

La Siguanaba was so happy. She wanted to ask his forgiveness, and use this wonderful opportunity to move to Washington D.C. and live in the White House.

El Cadejo was taken aback. He saw President Cipitio as his ticket out of poverty. He imagined getting a green card and being legit enough for a job as head of his son's Secret Service detail.

He hoped his son had designed an immigration reform bill that Congress would accept. President Cipitio had achieved peace in the Middle East and almost world peace, but the Republicans refused to support any kind of bill regarding immigration.

El Cadejo thought about helping his son to pass a reform bill, since it would benefit him personally. He liked the idea of not having to pay the penalties. His son could get him a break.

El Cadejo was always trying to scam the system. When he did not get his way, he ate the person. The motherfucker was crazy.

The big day arrived. El Cadejo and La Siguanaba were invited to visit their son at the White House. They were nervous.

President Cipitio was more nervous. He had to request medicinal marijuana to smoke a few joints before meeting the biological parents he hated. Not having parents had driven him to overachieve and over-compensate.

He had a plan. He greeted them and pretended to be happy when deep down inside was a powerful resentment.

El Cadejo came in disguise, looking very distinguished like Ricardo Montalban. He even spoke like him. The White House staff and press corps was in awe of his grace and eloquence. They did not realize they were dealing with a demon.

The President had a great strategy to get rid of his parents. He ordered Homeland Security to deport El Cadejo, saying the laws of the land must be followed.

He felt sorry for his mother and let her stay in the US, but at a menial job. She worked for the governor of Virginia as a house keeper. La Siguanaba soon rose to be in charge of the laundry services for the Hotel and Restaurant Association of Virginia. She was promoted because she knew that the wife of the Governor was having an affair with the gardener. Her promotion was given to La Siguanaba to keep her quiet. She no longer had to roam the villages and *quebradas* of her home country. Instead, she was the boss of laundry services and had a staff to wash the tablecloths and bed sheets and other material from the hotels and restaurants. Big machines did the hard work.

La Siguanaba stood and barked orders. She acted just like the previous bosses she used to have – the dictatorial type of bosses. She did not want to show any sense of favoritism or weakness. She thought to herself "I have suffered so much and now I will make others suffer. To make them stronger and resilient." It was also a method to gain respect and to be feared as a boss.

In the meantime, the news of El Cadejo being deported

83

back to El Salvador hit like wildfire. President Cipitio did not realize that he had unleashed a demon that was so angry that he summoned the spirits that lived within the Central American volcanoes. The local people knew them as the volcanoes of the undead.

The *Washington Post* broke the story, with its front-page headline read: President Cipitio's Father Deported.

Pro-immigrant rights groups were outraged and protested. Vigils and fasts were held in front of the White House.

The President was unmoved. Homeland Security was simply doing their job and he did not want to give any preferential treatment.

El Cadejo envied and hated his son. His goal was to unleash a nightmare for the President by destroying his peace process and achievements in Latin America.

On his return, El Cadejo developed alliances with different political groups, Democrats, Republicans, Independents and Greens, and various drug cartels from Mexico, Colombia, and the United States biggest cartels. Of course, the U.S. cartels used corporations as fronts. He created the alliances to overthrow the governments.

The motherfucker was crazy.

President Cipitio tracked how his father had unleashed chaos, hatred, and violence through Mexico and Central America. El Cadejo was the key advisor and consultant to the Mexican, Colombian, and US drug cartels. The fool was savvy, and signed on as an informant for the DEA.

The outraged President was in danger of all his work ruined, along with his legacy. He wanted El Salvador to build the biggest statue of him in honor of his achievements. President Cipitio wanted to be bigger than *Monumento al Divino Salvador del Mundo*. He wanted to replace the monument with his image.

Unofficially, El Cadejo declared war on his son. The President had to resort to his extraordinary non-human powers.

He had to fight evil with evil.

President Cipitio started covert operations. He asked his death squad to search and kill El Cadejo.

Twelve men and one woman were recruited. There nicknames were Cabron, Pitufo, Demonio, Mevale, Chingao, Bala, Soberbio, Rebelde, Granada, Poder, Chancletas, and the female's nickname was La Gata. The woman had to track, find, and seduce El Cadejo.

In the meantime, thousands of innocent civilians were tortured and murdered by El Cadejo and his thugs.

He roamed the streets in his true image: a wild, demonic half dog and half wolf with bloodshot eyes. The squad could find him by seeing his bright, bloody red eyes.

CHAPTER 14

IN EL SALVADOR AND HONDURAS, PRESIDENT CIPITIO'S death squad members partied like it was 1999. This was a big Prince song in 1982 but El Cipitio would play it as background music and required his death squad members to become fans of Prince before they would conduct subversive operations.

The underworld parties paid off. An informant told them he was one of the bodyguards of El Cadejo, and he was hiding deep down inside *El Volcan de Guazapa*.

The President's men and woman knew the location of their target. They requested the most sophisticated weaponry to permanently destroy El Cadejo. This was such advanced weaponry that the Pentagon designated each weapon as national security secrets. Some of the bullets within the weapons were filled the Ebola disease. To destroy El Cadejo with the Ebola virus.

Only President Cipitio knew how to restrain the demonic spirit of El Cadejo. He wanted El Cadejo captured and flown to Guantanamo Bay for torture.

The thirteenth member of the death squad was extremely hot. They knew El Cadejo's taste in women. He liked them voluptuous and dark skinned, and she fit the bill perfectly. She met him at a bar in La Gran Via de San Salvador. They partied and had a wonderful time. She even did lines of cocaine with El Cadejo.

Once he was fucked up, she requested a taxi and asked

to be taken to El Princess Hotel. She whispered promises in his ear that she would make him squeal like a little pig with joy. El Cadejo was so fucked up with alcohol and cocaine that he agreed. The weed they smoked also help slow his logical thinking processes and he suffered from schizophrenia. He could hear voices in his head.

They entered the room to find the other twelve members of the death squad waiting. The squad struggled with El Cadejo, since he had extraordinary strength even when loaded. Finally, they subdued his ass.

El Cadejo was tied up and flown to Guantanamo Bay. A special operations unit of the death squads, led by the top U.S. military General, known as Mr. Nails. The special operations unit conducted genetic tests and a psychological profile while torturing El Cadejo. They poured acid in his ears, poked his eyes with needles, and they loved electricquiting his testicles. They loved the smell of fried meat that came from his balls.

They kept El Cadejo as a prisoner in a steel cage. He was monitored twenty-four hours a day, seven days a week.

President Cipitio was not thinking of reelection time. He had to consolidate his power and the thirteen death squad members were fucking efficient. All he had to do was give them the name and possible address of their target. They took care of the hits right away.

He won the reelection easily and made the United States into the most powerful nation in the world. He did not use violence to gain obedience from other world leaders. He had mythical powers and an image like Gandalf from *The Lord of the Rings*.

Things rolled along with La Cholita.

The President filled out the last four years of his term of office without much controversy. Instead of retiring, he started a yoga class that eventually led to a world movement.

He admired Buddha and the Dalai Lama. He wanted to be revered as a saint, almost godlike. He wanted to be bigger than Chairman Mao.

El Cipitio created the Dim Sun Yoga Academy. That shit went worldwide. The little fucker became a yoga guru and millions signed up. El Cipitio used his physical and mental powers to convince members to join.

He could levitate, cure the ill, and sing songs while being in the most intricate yoga positions.

Slowly he had enough money to be a billionaire, actually the wealthiest little fucker, above Warren Buffet and Bill Gates. He became the first trillionaire in the world, with over six billion members of the Dim Sun Yoga Academy. Most of them paid by monthly debit payments and signed contracts to be official lifetime members. The contracts were not allowed to be broken. In fine print, the contract stated that if a member chose to leave, their homes, cars, and lifetime earnings were taken.

The Dim Sun Yoga Academy got the idea from the San Mateo County Department of Child Support Services. Poor fathers were fucked. They had to pay child support on a monthly basis for eighteen years. When they complained, they were fucked even more. San Mateo County was allowed to take away teaching or work credentials from deadbeat dads, and driver's licenses were suspended by the DMV. The goal was to crush the poor fathers by taking their means of work and transportation, to punish them for being unemployed.

But El Cipitio was content. He no longer had to work, or his family. La Cholita became a life-long member of the Dim Sun Yoga Academy.

He came from a developing country and ghetto to be a trillionnaire. No immigrant had ever achieved such success.

El Cipitio decided to donate his wealth to the poor children of the world. He was once that *descalzo, lleno de lombrices y piojos* child. He was one of them. He knew how it was to go to bed hungry. He knew the reality, beyond movies or books.

He now gave away his wealth to help others. He followed Mao, Buddha, and Jesus Christ's example of humility and helping thy neighbor.

El Cipitio roamed the streets of downtown Los Angeles, Hollywood, South Central, South East LA to remember his humble roots. Every other corner had a Dim Sun Yoga Academy, where they taught inner peace and joy.

His statue replaced the Salvador del Mundo in El Salvador,

the US decided to stick his image on the Statue of Liberty, and China erected a statue of El Cipitio in the middle of Tiananmen Square. Brazil exchanged their iconic Christ the Redeemer statue with one of El Cipitio. He was more popular than soccer legend Pele.

Some of his dreams became a reality: to be bigger than Chairman Mao, establish world peace, and to take naps.

That is some ironic shit. He could establish peace in the Middle East and Los Angeles, but he could not bring his own people in El Salvador to stop killing each other.

He knew the violence came from the colonization and brutality of the Spanish.

Wars existed among rival indigenous tribes, and the Cold War made Central America a hot spot. The political ideologies created much hatred.

Bringing the Dim Sun Yoga Academy to Central America did not work, and since peperecha bread was invented there, the population was immune to the ingredients that promoted peace.

He had gotten rid of El Cadejo, but the true root cause of the current violence was his own flesh and blood. The twin brother he had never known, El Duende.

To know his past, present, and future, El Cipitio searched for his brother. He had to confront his own self, and his own self-hatred.

The meeting might help him fill the void that money, power, and women never filled. He had all the money and power he ever dreamed about. He had La Cholita.

But he did not have a *familia*. Any conversation with his brother promised to be difficult.

To make a big splash, El Cipitio called Oprah and asked her to help him find his brother. She said, "Of course, my dear." Her producers went to work and traveled to Central America in search of El Duende. Oprah agreed that she would air a special live show just for El Cipitio.

El Cipitio asked for strict confidentiality.

Six months later, Oprah called with the news her people had found El Duende in La Higuera, Bolivia, where Che Guevara had been captured, tortured, and murdered. El Duende was enraged that the hands of El Che were chopped off via the orders of the Bolivian military, anti Castro Cuban operatives, and CIA agents.

Oprah was fascinated with the story of El Cipitio's brother and anticipated a boost to her ratings tremendously, especially since it concerned the former Mayor of Los Angeles and President of the United States, and world peace advocate, El Cipitio.

El Cipitio needed his brother to establish inner peace and establish a peace agreement between the MS 13 and Eighteen Street gangs in Central America. Only two people had the power to do so: El Cipitio and El Duende.

Oprah Winfrey was excited. She knew the problems and joys waiting for El Cipitio.

Oprah asked, "Does your brother speak English?" El Cipitio started to laugh and answered, "Hell yeah."

The date for the show was set and El Cipitio was nervous. He was about to meet his other half.

He wore a tailored black silk suit.

El Duende was not told about meeting El Cipitio. He wore a white silk suit for John Travolta's swagger and confidence in *Saturday Night Fever*. El Duende thought he was being recruited for an audition to be on *Soul Train*.

El Duende had a huge ego and was a self-proclaimed narcissist like his brother. He also had other conditions such as paranoia; since he had been a target since birth, this made sense.

He never knew La Siguanaba had given him away. He had grown up an orphan in the Catholic Church. He was thankful to the nuns who raised him. He grew up with hundreds of other orphan children.

He never knew his background but he knew he was born with extraordinary powers similar to El Cipitio, but El Duende had a small penis. His power lay within the gray matter of his brain. It was larger than most human beings. He had an IQ higher than Albert Einstein, and without the opportunities of an academic education or professional job.

He was short, three and a half feet tall, with a flat belly and light-skinned. El Duende looked like a dwarf creature and could see into the future. He dreamed about a lost brother, but never believed it was true.

El Duende drank Izze Sparkling Clementine Soda. The taste reminded him of the Orange Crush *gaseosas* back in El Salvador.

Instead of *guineos mahonchos*, his favorite fruit were mangos. He was pure and kind, yet also cursed with the genes of El Cadejo.

Oprah announced the interview with former President Cipitio for over a month, for an exclusive look at "Where are they now."

She bought a new sofa for El Cipitio and El Duende to sit close to each other. The sofa had to be smaller to make them look taller. She did not want their feet to be swinging above the floor.

The background had to look natural. She ordered fresh flowers. She wanted El Cipitio to feel comfortable for the cameras.

The big day came. A limousine brought El Cipitio alone. El Duende arrived riding a motorcycle. He wanted to show himself as a wild child. He even wore his black Harley Davidson boots with his white suit.

They went to separate green rooms for make-up. Oprah stopped by to say hello to each man. She was enthusiastic.

El Cipitio sat on the sofa and the first five minutes of the show started with Oprah talking to him, to catch up with what he was doing. Then she clued in the audience. She said, "We are here today so former President Cipitio can finally meet his lost twin brother." The audience gasped. The U.S. had more than one international hero.

El Duende sat with Oprah next to a short stranger. He felt a weird intuition that El Cipitio was someone from his dreams, from birth.

El Cipitio hugged El Duende and told him, *"Yo soy tu hermanito."* They embraced and cried uncontrollably. Neither had shown their emotions and soft side in public before.

They saw each other's tattoos. El Cipitio had "MS 13" on his left hand and El Duende had "18th Street" on his right hand.

Oprah gave them tissues to dry their eyes.

She asked questions and they answered. The audience and television viewers were mesmerized. Then El Cipitio asked El Duende, "Do you know who your parents were?" and El Duende said no.

El Cipitio told him their father was an evil, wicked man locked away forever. Their mother ran the largest laundry service in Virginia and Maryland and received psychiatric care for the decades of mistreatment and torture.

He asked his brother for a favor. "Why don't we sign a peace agreement to end the bloodshed between MS 13 and 18th Street?"

El Duende said, "I am willing to do it." The audience burst into applause. The numbers of viewers for the episode surpassed one billion. The agreement also included to stop killing innocent civilians and to stop murdering police officers from the Policia Nacional Civil (PNC) that were simply doing their jobs to support their families.

Taking a sheet of paper from the inside pocket of his tailored black silk suit, El Cipitio read the peace agreement he had previously prepared. All they had to do was sign and the violence in Central America would be over. They were both upset that the U.S. had purposely deported thousands of gang members who belonged to MS 13 and 18th Street. Once deported, these gang bangers created much chaos and violence in Mexico and Central America.

El Duende read the document. "You forgot a comma," he said, and they laughed. They placed their arms on each other shoulders. To show unity and love.

After the show, the brothers had a lot of catching up to do. They agreed to help protect and rebuild developing countries, and promote peace and nonviolence.

The brothers signed the agreement without having the United States or United Nations intervene. It was their responsibility to bring peace to Central America. They were sick and tired of the senseless violence.

The citizens of Panama, Belize, Costa Rica, Guatemala, El Salvador, Honduras, and Nicaragua erupted in joy. Millions of people walked the streets with no fear. They held parades. They did not have to pay extortion, or fear riding the buses. Peace meant they could go to work and come back home safely.

It was bigger than the ending of the civil wars of the 1980s. The peace agreement signed by the mero meros of MS 13 and 18th Street had to be notarized to make it official. Cecil King, a public notary in California, came with his official seal.

It was done. Peace was brought to Central America. Gangsters put their weapons down. No more murders were sanctioned or approved because of El Cipitio and El Duende. They had the same blood, and brothers and sisters should not kill each other.

Central America became prosperous. Imports and exports boomed. People were highly motivated to work. Millions of jobs were created and El Cipitio donated ninety-five percent of his wealth to build schools and hospitals, and establish Starbucks throughout the seven countries.

He created millions of jobs. Former gang members were hired as baristas for Starbucks. They loved the pay, benefits, vacation, and free air conditioning. El Cipitio paid them $20 per hour. They were extremely happy and no longer had to steal, bribe, torture, and kill to make a living.

Each country elected young presidents, male and female. These officials did not steal from their own treasuries. They were paid very well to be efficient presidents. El Cipitio provided seminars and workshops on effective leadership.

El Duende became an economic advisor to the countries. His IQ was so tremendous that he resolved major social challenges with one-page proposals, and the government assemblies and presidential administrations unanimously adopted his solutions. For example, he recommended for public school districts to provide top quality teachers for every school. He also made arrangements for all the fast food restaurants and hotels to donate their left over food to the homeless. He recommended for police departments to create jobs for parolees and ex-offenders so that they would not have to return to prison.

The Central American Economic Integration Commission (CAEIC) was created for the different countries to help each other through fair trade.

They competed with Europe and were partners with Asian and African nations.

People could not believe the prosperity resulting from the peace agreement signed by the brothers.

El Duende wanted to build soccer training schools and soccer fields, and offer small homes to the working poor. He asked El Cipitio to lend him the money to launch the Duende Foundation. Soon it was bigger than the Gates Foundation.

Through his foundation, El Duende also created refugee community centers throughout Mexico; Central Americans children and their parents stayed there while en route to the United States.

The brothers inherited kindness from their mother.

El Duende chose not to reunite with his mother, even though he had forgiven her. He remained angry that she gave him away and tried to drown his brother. Guilt from her decision to spare his life based on his light skin stayed with him.

The brothers made a pact to forgive their father, mother, and the adults that taught them how to torture, kill, and destroy. They hated having the evil gene from their father and agreed they had a problem, and continually sought spiritual healing.

They learned to trust with each other. El Duende wanted to meet La Cholita since his brother was madly in love with her.

The evil and extraordinary powers they inherited from their father, El Cadejo were kept a secret. No one should ever know the truth, they said, not even La Cholita.

La Siguanaba had already warned El Cipitio not to talk about the family curse with anyone.

However, El Cipitio and El Duende soon had the shock of their lives.

CHAPTER 15

E L CADEJO ESCAPED FROM EL VOLCAN DE GUAZAPA AND roamed the volcanoes of the undead, and began to visit the villages.

Children disappeared.

A wild creature was on the loose in El Salvador, Honduras, Guatemala, Nicaragua, and Belize.

In the tremendous panic, parents sent their children to the US by bus, train, and even walking to get to safety. They migrated in the hundreds of thousands.

El Cadejo roamed as far as Mexico and parts of the US. He was called *La Chupa Cabra*. Claims of photographs and videos were false; the real demon was too elusive. El Cadejo returned to form partnerships with the drug and human trafficking cartels.

He remained an evil spirit. He spread a rumor through the seven countries of Central America that the United States provided asylum for children. He purposely promoted violence and chaos so he could profit in trafficking humans. He loved for the violence to continued. He took great joy in hearing of torture, mass murders, leading to mass graves in Central America and Mexico.

He made millions of dollars. His greed, selfishness, and self-centered interests had not diminished.

El Cipitio and El Duende joined forces to destroy El Cadejo.

They faxed a letter to the Pope at the Vatican asking for the services of the best priest to conduct an exorcism. The brothers took the route of exorcising El Cadejo in the hope his evil spirit would be destroyed forever. They figured it worth a shot.

El Cadejo had to be seduced out of hiding. He loved Mexican *mole* and the City of Los Angeles was hosting a big mole festival.

El Cipitio contacted his old bodyguards and hired private investigators to track El Cadejo to the festival. He hogged the mole. He loved the black mole, pumpkin seed mole, and chicken mole. His favorite was the one made in Oaxaca.

As he ate his food, El Cadejo became drowsy. The private investigators and bodyguards had stirred *dormilona* pills into the mole. He fell into a deep sleep. They carried him away, telling the crowd, *"Esta borracho este pinche guey."*

El Cipitio was informed his father had been captured and taken to Guantanamo Bay, and he was ecstatic. He brought with him a secret weapon.

He had great joy in psychologically and physically torturing El Cadejo, the evil one. El Cipitio loved pouring salt and hot chile on open wounds. This reminded him of when he would pour salt of snails. He loved to see them squirm in pain. He was sadictic, just like his father that he detested.

El Cipitio showed his father a deep *olla*. He said, "I am going to cook *sopa de pata,* and you are the main ingredient."

The olla was filled with holy water from *La Placita Olvera* in downtown Los Angeles. The priest, Padre Santo, sent by the Pope helped with the process.

When the sopa de pata was burning hot, they dumped in his ass. El Cadejo fought but the holy water was too powerful.

His meat softened and other ingredients were added. Five different caserolas and ollas cooked the different ingredients. When the sopa was ready, El Cipitio, the priest, and the bodyguards ate El Cadejo. This was the only way to absorb and destroy his evil spirit. The exorcism worked as the evil spirit was expelled from his body. They could not resist the splashes of holy water. It was so fucking cold that they could not stand it and they were forced to leave El Cadejo's tortured body.

El Cipitio defeated his own father by torturing, cooking, and eating the sopa de pata. He said that it was the best ever. He even requested *una sopa de chipilin*. The smell of the soups were alluring and powerful.

The brothers became the most powerful motherfuckers around. They dedicated themselves to do good in the world and fight evil at all levels.

El Cipitio asked El Duende not to tell La Siguanaba because she was *chambrosa* and would tell everyone. She was so chambrosa she would likely tell her staff and *patrones*.

El Cadejo was gone and El Cipitio and El Duende could sleep at night.

El Duende decided to take a break. He joined Las Cruces monastery in New Mexico to regain his sanity.

He used the knowledge he gained at the monastery to teach others about peace, love, tolerance, and compassion. He wanted to be the Salvadoran Dalai Lama and end racism, and influence mediocre comedians like Paul Rodriguez to accept Central American immigrant children. Rodriguez had gone on CNN Live and recommended the refugee children be deported, even though he was an immigrant from Mexico with a big *nopal* on his forehead. The comic was like the assimilated Chicanos who hated Mexican immigrants. Also, a few Salvadorans were becoming anti-immigrant. El Duende hated *vendidos*, the sellouts.

El Duende convinced the President of the United States, nicknamed President Hope, to sign an executive order giving legal residency to over 90,000 Central American refugee children. The children now had a chance to be future leaders of America. While his brother implemented those incredible humanitarian actions, El Cipitio wondered if he should have children with La Cholita. He worried about his children inheriting some of the genes from El Cadejo. But he wanted to settle down.

The brothers joined former President Jimmy Carter with his *Habitat for Humanity* efforts. They built homes in the poorest villages around the world and were truly at peace. La Cholita chose to emulate her hero, Mother Teresa. She began to feed the most needy and she took care of the terminally ill. She showed unconditional love for everyone. She treated everyone with kindness and love.

El Cipitio did good deeds for about a year or two. He chose to recycle and he gave the proceeds to the Boys and Girls Club. He also volunteered at public schools with tutoring.

He wondered what his next steps should be in achieving his dreams.

He daydreamed. He wanted to help establish world peace and prosperity for everyone.

El Salvador suffered a humiliating defeat when they played against Hungary in the 1982 Fédération Internationale de Football Association (FIFA) World Cup held in Spain.

They lost the game ten to one.

El Cipitio wanted revenge, either as El Salvador's coach or a key forward player. His goal was to take El Salvador to the upcoming FIFA World Cup in China and win it.

Salvadoran beach soccer players were some of the best in the world. He recruited the players to the national soccer team, bought them Nike tennis shoes, and inspired and trained them to become world champions.

They could win the World Cup if they set their minds to it. El Cipitio had to pay the players well in order to avoid corruption, since many of the players were used to taking bribes to lose games on purpose.

The Salvadoran Soccer Federation did not pay enough and many of the professional players had to do odd jobs in order to survive during the offseason. Sometimes the Soccer Federation could not pay the players because the money had been stolen; they agreed to be part of the corruption to eat.

El Cipitio knew the corruption in the FIFA had spread among the referees. He increased the salaries of the referees so they did not participate in the bribes. With a fair playing field, the developing countries had a chance at winning the World Cup finals.

But he wanted to take a break and recuperate mentally and physically. He retreated with La Cholita and lived under the radar for a year or two. Volunteering with Habitat for Humanity had shown him the living conditions of the poor throughout the world.

He had to resist his evil and wicked side and fight his evil urges. Every day he restrained himself from imagining tortures. El Cipitio wanted to overcome his violent genetics. He figured that if he sacrificed and suffered enough, he would be cleansed of his sins.

He wanted to give his live in service to others. He already had achieved much in his life as Mayor of Los Angeles and President of the United States.

The deep hole in his soul needed to be filled. Lying in bed with La Cholita at night, he still felt extraordinarily lonely.

Ultimately, the focus of El Cipitio's life had shrunk to the eternal question, "Who am I?" He only knew superficially who he was.

The Dim Sun Yoga Academy had helped him connect his body with his mind and soul, but he remained a lost soul.

Renouncing his addictions and sins was a lifelong struggle.

He learned from Buddha, Allah, and Jesus Christ, and emulated those great leaders. They were true revolutionaries with great zeal, who had convinced billions of people to follow and revere them.

He wanted that inner peace, calmness, and self-love.

El Cipitio soon had two part-time jobs, one at Starbucks and another one at a car wash during the weekends. He rode an orange bike to both jobs. Gasoline was too expensive.

He wanted a simple and peaceful life. He thought about going into rehab, but he said to himself, *fuck that shit.*

To relax, he lit up a joint and decided to play *Can't Get Enough of Your Love, Babe* by Barry White, while he drifted into a deep sleep. El Cipitio began to teleport into his next adventures.

TRANSLATION - *DEFINITIONS*

renta/rent = *extortion money*

cooperativas/cooperatives = *small businesses set up to provide small loans for agricultural entrepreneurs*

maciso/massive/strong = *in reference to a tough guy – like an oak tree*

mierda/shit = *as in holy shit*

huerfanos/orphans = *from here nor there*

semillas de marañón = *cashew seeds*

bolas = *money*

agua de coco = *coconut water*

kola shampan = *traditional salvadoran soda that is now foreign owned*

campesino = *caretaker of the land*

salvadoreño americano = *salvadoran american*

soy el cipitio = *i am el cipitio*

quebrada = *stream of water/small river*

guineo majoncho = *tropical banana*

cantones = *small rural villages – within nature outskirts*

hijos de puta = *sons of bitches*

pipiles = *indigenous of el salvador*

101

guardia nacional = *national guard*

queso duro = *hard cheese*

guardia civil = *civil guard*

la matanza = *the killings/the massacre/genocide*

futbol = *soccer*

platanos fritos = *fried plantain*

pinche = *typical mexican term used to refer to others in a derogatory manner*

porque me aogaste = *why did you drown me?*

porque eres el demonio = *because you are a demon*

lombrises = *tapeworms*

frijoles monos = *beans – typical salvadoran food*

sandias = *watermelons*

jocotos, marañónes, chipilines = *typical salvadoran fruits and vegetable used to cook a succulent soup*

enamorado = *eternally in love/deeply in love*

mierda! dolor de cabeza = *shit, headache*

el negro = *blackie*

gringos = *white people*

estos hijos de puta me las pagaran = *these sons of bitches will one day pay the price*

se llevaron a los cipotes = *they took the children*

mestizos = *mixture of european and indigenous blood*

indios = *indians/native americans/indigenous*

estos indios ignorantes y rebeldes = *these ignorant and rebellious indians*

el cacique = *the big cheese, the big boss, landowner*

comando urbano = *urban commander*

el cherito = *little friend, little homie*

comandantes = *the commanders*

mara salvatrucha = *gang created in hollywood/los angeles*

puro cuello = *influence & access through connections/relatives*

mero mero = *the main one*

cipotas = *girls/women*

mire jefecito, como le corte los dedos y las orejas = *look boss, how I cut their fingers and ears*

le pego el cipote = *impregnated with male kid*

mujeriego = *womanizer*

el norte = *the north – the united states*

un chingon = *tough motherrfucker*

a la gran puta & hijo de la puta = *the big bitch and son of a bitch*

mil mascaras = *thousands masks*

federales = *mexican police – known to be corrupt*

colones = *original salvadoran currency*

menudo = *traditional mexican soup*

guanaco = *derogatory terms used against salvadorans*

polleros & coyotes = *mostly corrupt guides and exploiters of immigrants.*

sopa de frijoles con carne = *bean soup with chunks of meat*

supremas & regias = *traditional salvadoran beers*

indio atlacatl = *indigenous pipil/mayan warrior/leader.*

cholos = *gangbangers with an attitude*

mojado = *wetback*

chaparro = *shorty*

goma = *hangover*

cholitas = *female gang bangers*

enamorando = *romancing*

enamorado eterno = *eternally in love*

el poeta sin barrio = *the poet with no hood'*

cholos pelones = *bald headed gang bangers*

placa = grafitti - *name on a wall*

morra – su ruca = *a female / his woman*

ese = *referring to someone who is down*

la eme = *mexican mafia*

paletero = *ice cream vendor*

burrito de carne asada = *steak burrito*

horchata = *traditional salvadoran drink*

el mercado central = *central market where stabbings and bad words are common. strong smell of cheese.*

platanos with frijoles and crema = *fried plantain with cream*

conquistadores = *conquerors*

cuches = *traditional salvadoran words meaning pigs/porks*

puercos = *pigs*

una peperecha = *a traditional salvadoran sweet bread & can also serve as a code word for whore*

mariposa = *butterfly – pokes around*

cinturita de gallina = *fine ass chicken waist*

querida = *my love*

la cholita = *the gangster*

ojos que no ven – corazon que no siente = *eyes that don't see – a heart that does not feel*

panzon, quebadro, tornillo, and truco = *big belly, broke ass, screw, and tricky*

la malinche = *traitor to her own people*

el presidente de estados unidos = *the president of the united states*

torta = *popular mexican food*

pupusa = *popular salvadoran food*

juan gabriel = *mexican singer*

que necesita compadre = *what do you need compadre*

pues que chingado – una pinche acta de nacimiento = *fuck, just a fucking birth certificate*

no hay pedo – solo cien bolas y se la tenemos mas tarde = *no big fucking deal – just one hundred bucks and we will have it later*

me hizo soñar y cree que yo podia ser un tailor en beverly hills = *you made me believe that I could become a tailor in beverly hills*

chota = *the police*

que viva la revolucion = *long live the revolution*

frijolero = *beaner*

caserola = *pan*

olla = *pot*

sopa de res or sopa de pata = *beef soup and cow feet soup*

azucar – mi cipitio tiene tumbao = *sugar – my cipitio has swag*

el jefe = *the boss*

el cipitio tiene corazon = *el cipitio has heart*

monumento al divino salvador del mundo = *monument of the divine saviour of the world*

el volcan de guazapa = *giant volcano located in el salvador*

descalzo, lleno de lombrices y piojos = *barefoot, full of tape worms and lice*

salvador del mundo = *saviour of the world*

gaseosas = *sodas*

yo soy tu hermanito = *I am your little brother*

dormilona = *sleeping pills*

esta borracho este pinche guey = *this fool is hella drunk*

la placita olvera = *allegedly where los angeles was founded. some say los angeles was founded at the san gabriel mission area*

sopa de chipilin = *traditional salvadoran soup*

nopal = *cactus*

vendidos = *sell outs*

CPSIA information can be obtained
at www.ICGtesting.com
Printed in the USA
FSOW01n1748101214
3785FS